A Noble INTENT

CORNERSTONE SERIES | Book 12
KENDALL HOXSEY

A Noble
INTENT

A Noble Intent

Cornerstone Series #12

Published by Beyond the Bookery

Copyright 2025 by Kendall Onysko

A Noble Intent by Kendall Onysko 2025

Cover Design: Mountain Peak Edits & Design

Edited by: Beacon Editing and MadLit Assist

All Rights Reserved

ASIN: B0D1ZJ2GB8

ISBN: 9798306973753

No part of this publication may be reproduced or rewritten, stored on a digital device outside of the original product, or transmitted in any form or by any means, electronic, paper, audio, or otherwise without the prior written permission of the author.

The only exception is brief quotations in reviews for promotional purposes by readers, reviewers, bloggers, or book influencers.

This book is a work of fiction. Names, characters, places, settings, and incidents are the product of the author's imagination or are used fictitiously in the telling of this story. Any resemblance to true events, locations, or persons, living or dead, is coincidental.

No AI training: Without in any way limiting the author's exclusive rights under the copyright, any use of this publication to "train" generative artificial intelligence (AI) technologies to generate text is expressly prohibited. The author reserves all rights to license uses of this work for generative AI training and development of machine learning language models.

CORNERSTONE SERIES

A Noble Purpose Laurie Lucking	A Noble Past Anna Augustine
A Noble Match Kirsten Fichter	A Noble Warrior Lucy Peterson
A Noble Grace E.G. Bella	A Noble Loyalty Olivia Godfrey
A Noble Heart Jewel Windall	A Noble Intent Kendall Hoxsey
A Noble Princess Saraina Whitney	A Noble Rescuer K.R. Mattson
A Noble Companion Rachel Kovaciny	A Noble Life C.K. Heartwing
A Noble Assassin Abigail Kay Harris	A Noble Friend Kendra E. Ardnek
A Noble Protector Madisyn Carlin	A Noble Comfort Katja H. Labonté

LEARN MORE AT WWW.BEYONDTHEBOOKERY.COM

Jeff- Loving you has given my life and heart so much joy. From the moment, over 12 years ago, when you told me you watched Jane Eyre so you could understand what I loved about it, I knew you were a keeper. Even though reading is not one of your passions, I will forever adore you for that gesture.

You push me to be better in all things and even when I'm ready to retreat, you are there to rally my spirits and help me forge ahead. I don't know how to accurately thank God for bringing you into my life. Always know I'm grateful for your love, support, and the life we've built together as husband and wife. And our precious little ones, Lizzie and Jack. Thank you for taking on the role of husband and father with your wholehearted devotion. This life and our family is infinitely more than I deserve.

I knew when I was creating Prince Max there were many traits borrowed from you. Your determination, sense of right and wrong, and many other character traits. But let's face it I'm also a sucker for your handsome face. More than anything it is long past time to dedicate a novella to you ;-) After all, I wouldn't have completed the past two novellas without you. I love you, guapo. Always.

Contents

1. Chapter 1   1
2. Chapter 2   13
3. Chapter 3   24
4. Chapter 4   34
5. Chapter 5   45
6. Chapter 6   56
7. Chapter 7   67
8. Chapter 8   77
9. Chapter 9   87
10. Chapter 10   97

About the author   108

Acknowledgements   109

Also by Kendall Hoxsey   111

Chapter 1

Once upon a time...

My family ruled the kingdom of Cadmium. From the northern islands to the southern deserts, and the eastern cliffs of Acillion to the western edges of the Evernight Forest. My grandfather, King Reinhard, died under mysterious circumstances. Lady Vermillion and her invading army captured and tortured my father, Ansgar. I, as a little boy, escaped with the Wolves, our elite tribe of warriors. Once they completed their training and swore a blood oath, they were wolves for life.

I've plotted my revenge against Lady Vermillion for over twenty years. The wolves and I hide out in the abandoned isles. She and her spies "the Huntsmen" have never found us. Throughout the isles are unmarked graves of her huntsmen. God will forgive me. I will restore order to this kingdom and then dedicate my life to His penitence. After I've avenged my family.

The gales surge from the west. My somewhat shaggy brown hair follows the wind and out of my eyes and the salty air steals any moisture from my lips. As I stood atop the cliffs the ominous black clouds loomed ever closer in the distance above the tumultuous sea. The waves beat against the rocky land below like a battle drum. Tonight begins it all. I will lead this storm into Cadmium. Right to Scarlet Castle. And to erase the reign of Lady Vermillion forever.

A whistle draws me from my musings.

One of the wolves leads his horse and mine towards me. "Prince Max, it's time to leave." Sir Ludovic presses the reins into my hands. My stallion, Deimhan, side steps and tosses his head. I patted his shank wanting to soothe him. I, too, am jittery and anxious for the journey ahead. But as the leader I won't show that I am feeling anything less than confident.

I check the saddle bags and am satisfied that all supplies are assembled. I mount and lead the wolves down the hill to the ship below. We will sail for the mainland and dock at a secret harbor.

"Spare your horse, Your Highness." Sir Marius called out. "The devil isn't on our heels yet."

I pull up on the reins, but Deimhan is as eager as I am to reach our destination. Years of scrounging, collecting information, training all to exact revenge.

We reach the ship and load. Each wolf finds a spot on the boat to sit down but my body and mind are too busy to relax. Blood flowed through my veins like a roaring current. Clenching my fists as I exhaled, I refocused on simple tasks. "Does the tailor have our costumes ready?"

One of the wolves elbowed Sir Kaspar, as the others smiled and gawked.

Knowing Kaspar's penchant for flirtation, I assumed that the tailor had a daughter. Eyes downcast with pink cheeks, Kaspar hands each of us, black felt face masks with black velvet coats, as the others gesture and tease about his exploits.

Trying not to roll my eyes, "I think we will stand out if we all have the same costume. The huntsmen will notice a group of men all dressed alike."

Most agree with me with grunts and nods.

Marius shakes his head. "With so many in attendance, I doubt anyone will actually notice us." My best friend. The only one to ever publicly disagree with me.

"Just because the huntsmen haven't found us all these years, does not mean we let our guard down. Especially when we are in their lair." I don't want any of the wolves to take unnecessary risks tonight. We are a pack and by extension my family. My only family now.

Marius walks over, smiling, and curls his hand on my shoulder. Playfully shaking it. "Relax, Your Highness. We'll sneak into the ball. Gather information. Sneak out and make our next move. No one will make any uncalculated move. Without your approval of course."

The corners of my mouth level back in mock annoyance. "Or without yours."

Marius chuckled and put on his coat. After tying his blonde hair into a queue, he reached a hand into his pocket and then held up five pieces of straw with tops all level.

"What is that for?" Marius often created games to occupy everyone, but I hesitated at the gleam in his expression.

"To choose which of us asks Lady Gisela for a dance." Marius smirked.

"Won't the huntsmen be guarding her?" Sir Kaspar sharpened his dagger with a black water stone.

"Yes, but she's also the only one able to read the ancient text. She's our best option to find the red diamond." Madius ensured no one cheated as they pulled their piece of straw.

"Well, if she is the only one then she must not be bright otherwise Lady Vermillion would already be declared Queen."

I chose last but I already knew luck is not with me tonight. I tugged my choice straw from his hands, and it kept coming and coming. My gut knew that Marius wanted me to be the one to ask Gisela to dance.

The others hooted with laughter and patted my shoulder. "Have fun, Your Highness."

They all dispersed around the ship to either sleep or play cards. "I've heard Lady Gisela is a great disappointment to Lady Vermillion. She is not a beauty and spends all her time in the library reading books."

I sat down and leaned back against the railing. Twirling the straw in my fingers, musing on the past. I remembered the little baby, Gisela, I'd met years ago. Auburn curls and a button nose. What kind of person did the baby become?

Marius sat beside me and nudged me with his elbow. "I had to Max."

I stared ahead, still miffed at him. "You could have shared your plan with me."

"You would never agree to dance with any maiden. Let alone Gisela."

"Do you really think she is the only one that can read the ancient text?"

"We have yet to find anyone who can."

I nod, knowing he's right. It's annoying how often he is right. I would rather kiss a scorpion than waste my time dancing. Especially with a woman related to Lady Vermillion even if Gisela is not personally responsible for the deaths of my family.

"Stop scowling and start to think of the fun you might have." Marius stands up, puts his hands on his hips and inclines his head towards the pack as he walks in their direction. "Come join us when you're ready."

Somehow, I know that fun is the last thing I will enjoy tonight. Lady Gisela is my blood enemy as the granddaughter of Lady Vermillion. Innocence is no excuse. I've lost my entire family to Lady V's machinations. Revenge is the only thing that keeps me going. I will avenge every single loved one. And I will make every member from the house of Vermillion pay with their lives if necessary.

~~~

The wolves and I traveled through the Evernight forest. No other soul dared to travel through it. Yet it is the quickest route to Scarlet Castle. At the edges of the forest, the mountains of Parpelia create a stunning vista of power. My great-great grandfather built the castle for his bride, Amytis. The turrets are often mistaken for mountain peaks. A hidden fortress built into the mountains. They all believed impenetrable. Until Lady V and her mercenaries, the Huntsmen, overtook the castle.

"Why did they name it Scarlet Castle?" Sir Kaspar nudged his horse to catch up to mine. As the youngest of the wolves, Kaspar often asked the most questions.

"My great-great grandfather placed in the highest tower the red diamond he claimed God gifted our family. When the sun rose in the morning and set at night the light would hit the diamond, and the red rays reached villages for miles."

"Wasn't he worried someone would steal it?" He held up his

"Apparently not. My grandfather told me that it was meant to show that God is everywhere. And the king should help share that light with his people."

"Do you think Lady V is hiding the red diamond?"

We halted our horses halfway up the mountain pass. More of the castle is visible with each yard we gain. My jaw tightens and my fingers clench on the reins.

I've considered every possibility. Lady V could have it, but she would make it known. She must think I have it. Otherwise, why would she send her huntsmen after me all these years? "No, Lady V doesn't have it."

"Why does the diamond matter?" Ludovic interjects. "We are strong enough to take on Lady V and her huntsmen."

"Because whoever possesses the red diamond is the king or queen of Cadmium. When God bestowed his gift, it was a pact. We as the wolves must honor that pact with God." Marius trots his horse close to mine. I think to show solidarity, but he worries about me too much.

I kick Deimhan to move ahead of the group so I can judge the distance we still need to travel. I hold up a closed fist. The wolves halt and we dismount to dress for the ball behind the castle stables.

Throughout the years, we intercepted messages from Lady V. Which were helpful in knowing her plans for the kingdom. Tonight, she wanted important people to attend the ball, promising a special announcement. *With such a carrot dangled in front of me, how could we not attend?* We entered the gates to the castle amidst the crowd. Not one guard questioned us. I breathed easier. Gaining entrance into the ball had been easier than I anticipated.

\#

I stumbled for the third time on the hem of my crimson velvet gown walking down the stairs to the ballroom. I loathed dressing up and smiling for grandmama's fake courtiers. As the crown princess I know I should love everything about a ball. The protocols, the dancing, the posturing, the gossip. No. Definitely, no thank you.

A library or the forest, that is where I wanted to be.

I reached the bottom without breaking an ankle and located Grandmama, across the room, lounging in her red brocade throne. She loved every minute of her parties. Her smile was large enough to reach from ear to ear and her eyes continually scanned the room. A line of subjects patiently waited to have their brief audience with the queen. But Grandmama kept glancing up and around the ballroom between conversations. Who was she looking for?

Walking slowly to not trip again, or worse, tear the dress, I hugged the stone wall, wanting to fade into the crowd. Most importantly to escape any unsolicited offers to dance. Reaching the third candelabra, I settle into the tiny alcove which also hides a secret passageway.

"I thought I'd find you here." A familiar voice whispered in my ear.

I turned to embrace my best friend, Selene.

Her ebony hair is twisted into a beautiful knot atop her head with a few tendrils dangling above her shoulders. Ever the belle of every ball. Grandmama has never said it, but she loathes Selene. Her eyes narrow and complains of a stomachache or headache whenever Selene is close by.

"Whom are you hiding from?" Selene smiled as she searched the faces of courtiers nearby for noted pedantic or stuffy ones.

"No one in particular." I threaded my arm through hers and we walked towards the back of the ballroom. The red silk curtains are tied back from the floor to ceiling windows that line the room. Life size topiary statues are staged throughout along with flower arrangements in silver and green urns.

~~~

The tiny hairs at the back of my neck stand up. I shiver not knowing why. Selene and Lina are looking beyond me with wide eyes. I turned and met a full muscular chest only inches from my face. "May I have this dance?" Tilting my head back to see a large black mask covering the upper half of his face. He puts his hand out palm and repeats his question in a deep, rough voice, "May I have this dance?" I'm mute, watching his hand hold steady waiting for mine. He stands at least a head taller than me. He is a stranger. I'm sure I've never seen him before. Before I could refuse, Lina volunteered me. "She'd love to."

I place my trembling fingers in his. As we walk towards the dance floor, I glare at Lina, hoping she will worry about retribution. We take our places amongst the dancers in two straight lines facing our partners. One lone horn played a minor B flat and then the violins, flutes, and violas slowly joined in, and the gentlemen promenaded towards their partners. I'm focused on performing the movements, not making small talk when he says, "You outshine all others tonight." I stepped on his foot and almost tripped, but he caught me and led me to follow the others as everyone linked arms.

I'm caught off guard and murmur, "thank you." Not knowing what else to say. I'm not a brilliant conversationalist. I know it is something Grandmama wished I were better at. Amongst many, many, other things.

He guides me to face him. I look up into his features once more. My throat went dry. His eyes hypnotized mine. Something about his dark hooded grey eyes like the early morning fog that shrouds the sun. His black face mask covers all other features. Underneath my hand on his shoulder is lean muscle. Each turn and step he guided me with agility. I had rarely danced before and never with a man who focused on me like he was a wolf stalking me, a deer.

His eyes shifted to look over my shoulder. He nodded but returned his attention back to me. "You dance well."

I scoff. "Please I rarely like flattery, much less false flattery."

One side of his mouth curves. "If you don't like flattery, what should a gentleman do to gain your attention?" He grabs my waist and lifts me up as all the other gentlemen do for their lady partners. My breath catches as my heartbeat quickens. I place my hands on his shoulders as he lowers me. My feet touch the floor, but my head thinks I'm still in the air. I was letting a pair of dark mesmerizing eyes affect me more than they should.

"I wouldn't know. Few men have tried to gain my attention."

His eyes widened but continued on with the steps. "I'm sorry for that."

"Why?"

"Because every woman deserves to have a man tell her she is beautiful."

I'm struggling to know what to say next. Not every woman thinks beauty is her only quality! "What is your name?"

"I'm no one of consequence."

"Lady Vermillion wouldn't have invited just anyone. Surely, you're just being modest." I peruse his stature. His hand tightens on mine. Specks of dirt showed underneath his nails, and while his hair is tied back into a queue, one piece hair is too short to stay confined and resided along his right temple.

"I hear you are a scholar. Yet you've never been able to read the ancient dragon text."

Who is this man? Why did he know that about me? My temper is also piqued with his casual insult. "For 'no one of consequence' you seem to know something no one else does about me. Only one other person was able to read and decipher that."

"Yes, your m—"

Trumpets sound, alerting the guests to pay attention Grandmama. Lina and Selene take my hands and lead me closer to the dais where Grandmama stands in front of her throne. To most in the audience Grandmama appears the image of calm and grace, but I know her pinched lips and threaded hands behind her back are not a good sign. Something or someone has upset her. I just hope it isn't me.

"It has been nearly twenty years since I began my reign. Despite my huntsmen's best-efforts Max and his wolves still menace the kingdom. They must be stopped. And I've decided that my granddaughter, Lady Gisela, will bring them to justice."

How would I do that? My skills were in deciphering texts and horseback riding. Hardly enough to track Prince Max and his wolves. Why was she sending me and not the Huntsmen? They were the warriors, not me. What made Grandmama think that I would be different? My mind whirls in a blur and I'm anxious to know what motive is behind this.

She gestures to her right. An elderly man with salt and pepper mutton chops and bifocals steps forward and stands close to Grandmama practically beaming. "Professor Gruden, from the university is an expert of the ancient books of Cadmium. He has recently deciphered a text describing the origins of this kingdom and what gives true authority to the ruler of this land."

My stomach turned queasy, and dread ate away at my stomach. Grandmama wanted our lineage to continue as the rulers of Cadmium forever. I had read every important text I could find. Nothing gave the answers. Grandmama had long since lost hope in me. "What good is your skill if it doesn't have the answers I need?"

What text had Professor Gruden found? Could Gruden have misinterpreted the text? Or did he have an alternative motive? Without saying a word to Selene or Lina I approach the dais. A hand closes on my forearm. My eyes tracked from the fingers up the arm to see the owner's face. Sir Hugo, the senior huntsman. Ever reliable and utterly devoted to Grandmama.

"Wait until she calls for you," he advises.

I expel a breath, knowing he is right. I should not cause any commotion, but waiting to ask questions seems harder.

"You must work on hiding your emotions."

My eyebrows lift.

"You want to charge in without thinking. Lady Vermillion knows that you are driven by your emotions. She'll make you wait because she can. Knowing it will upset you."

I nodded and turned away. My cheeks flamed with heat knowing I'm so easy to read.

"Tonight, we celebrate my reign and in three days' time we will all gather to wish Lady Gisela luck as she will finally bring an end to the House of Moritz."

After her speech, I scurry towards the dais, but the majordomo blocks my path. "Lady Vermillion says she will speak with you in the morning."

Dismissed once again. When will I learn to take advice?

\#

I caught Marius' attention across the ballroom. A few random guests milled around. The wolves cannot leave as a group. The huntsmen are not complete imbeciles.

I point towards the grandfather clock where we first entered. Once we reached our meeting point, I whispered. "Gather the men. We will meet back at the campsite. I have a new plan."

Guests pass by not paying much attention to us. Though a few young ladies glance at Marius. His blonde hair and stature did seem to appeal to ladies everywhere we traveled. I'm still cautious to speak above a whisper. "We are going to offer our services as guides to Lady Gisela."

Marius opens his mouth, his typical mirth gone. "Are you insane?"

For once, I'm the one smiling. I'm the one frustrating Marius. Rather than vice versa. "Not at all. And I'm going to convince Lady V to hire us first." Before Marius can further argue with me, I walk away not caring about his possible arguments.

With my plan solidifying in my mind, I'm eager to appraise the wolves.

I proved to myself that I could be in the same room as Lady V and disguise my identity. I held her granddaughter in my arms and didn't harm her. I smirk, recalling Gisela's small display of temper. I had fooled them all including Lady V, Hugo, the Huntsmen, and Gisela. A warm feeling pulsed through my veins. Luring them into my trap may not be as difficult as I anticipated.

Chapter 2

Convincing the wolves to let me meet with Lady V alone took every bit of my negotiating prowess. Each volunteered to take my place. No one was going to talk me out of this. I reminded Marius of his little game with straws, forcing me to dance with Gisela. I was the prince, and I accepted the responsibility and the danger. Convincing Lady V to hire me as Gisela's guide would require manipulation and covert skills. I couldn't allow anyone else to go in my stead.

"Max, let me go with you," Marius pleaded.

"No. Lady V may find you too charming and want you to be her newest favorite at court."

Marius shuddered.

"Let's try to stay out of any potential webs from that arachnid."

I left Deimhen with the wolves and borrowed a simple bay gelding from a blacksmith in one of the villages surrounding the castle.

As I stood in the receiving room, I considered Marius' parting words. "When you're talking to Lady V forget about who you really are. She is an expert at deception and filtering out information. Don't try to outsmart her right away."

My heartbeat raced and I sat in a chair in the corner. A dozen people filled the room, waiting for their audience with Lady V, fidgeting. I stared up at the ceiling trying to take a calming breath without giving away that I'm nervous. Black boots stop in front of me and a throat clears. I looked up to see the scribe, who printed my name to request an appointment. Over three hours ago.

"You may go in now." He sniffed and returned to his desk.

I entered a room of gold filigree wallpaper, satin pillows, and brocade curtains. After sleeping on the ground and using spare blankets for pillows anything would be ostentatious to me. I don't remember my grandfather's study looking like this. *The royal coffers must be empty if this is how she decorates.*

"Hurry up." A voice speaks from a corner. "I have many *important* matters to attend to."

Perfect. I annoyed her before opening my mouth. *Focus! This is your one chance!*

"Forgive me, Lady Vermillion!" I shuffled forward, lowered to my knees, and bowed. I kept my head down to act subservient. "The kingdom is abuzz with news of Lady Gisela's quest to find the lost diamond. I've come to humbly offer my services as a guide."

"Word travels fast." She quipped. "What is your name?"

"Rolf." I used a variation of one of my middle names.

"Why should I hire you when I have the huntsmen?"

"I know the location of the Owl."

Her eyebrows raise and quickly drop. She scanned me up and down with nothing moving but her eyes. "Who is your family?"

"We are mountain folk. Hunters from birth."

"You didn't answer my question."

"I lived in the mountain town of Rubine"

She snorted. "Traitors who supported the House of Moritz. Why should I trust you with my granddaughter?"

"Because I was the child that betrayed the town to your huntsmen."

Her lips pursed. "I was told he was dead."

I pretended to sneeze to hide my joy that she was taking the bait. "Your huntsmen left me in an abandoned well to die."

"You must have a strong will to survive." She picks up her cup and saucer to take a sip of her tea. "Besides that, what other skills qualify you to lead Gisela?"

"I know how to traverse all terrains and have couriered messages throughout the four corners of the kingdom."

"So have the huntsmen." With an exhalation, she moves her hand towards a small silver bell.

I dangle the ultimate carrot, one she cannot resist. "I also know the hideouts of Prince Max and his pack of wolves."

Her green eyes scrutinize me. I've got her full attention now. Like a black widow ready to kill the insect trapped in her web. A good hunter and reveled in seeking their prey. My sense of vengeance kept me alive all these years. It was time for her to be on the defensive.

"And how can I be sure that you're not one of them? Wanting to ransom Gisela once she leaves the castle?"

Marius was right about not trying to outwit her too much this first time.

I bow my head once more, showing her my faux subservience. "My lady, I betrayed the House of Moritz once before. Why wouldn't I do so again?"

"What do you expect as a reward?"

"I want to be a huntsman."

"That's all?" She scoffs.

She stands and brushes past me over to the desk. Her gown skimmed the floor with the foot-long train slithering in the grass. Every movement is elegant and measured giving the impression of inbred majesty. All an illusion.

As much as she makes my skin crawl, I understand how she lured my father into her web. She is an attractive woman but evil lies beneath her veneer of beauty.

The feather tip pen scratches against the parchment. She signs her name with generous loops and flourishes and blows softly on the parchment to dry the ink. As she walked around the desk to stand in front of me, I caught a whiff of Lady V's pungent, on the cusp of shriveling, floral scent. I remember how Gisela smelled of wildflowers.

Lady V holds out her hand. My stomach wants to protest but I focus on kissing her [descriptor] skin and promise to thoroughly scrub my lips later.

"I like handsome men to join the Huntsmen. If you do well in this task, I look forward to your personal protection."

"Yes, my lady." I take the scroll and bow again.

"Return here at three o'clock. I will introduce you to Gisela then."

I raced to the doors leading to the receiving room. And didn't stop until I reached the stables. I've gotten Lady V to believe my story and hire me as Gisela's guide. When I reach my horse, I find Kaspar hiding in the stall.

Furious that my order was disobeyed. I glared at him. "How long have you been here?"

"I just arrived, M—"

I sliced my fingers underneath my chin and checked around the stables to make sure we were alone. "My name is Rolf and if you're looking for a job, I am leading a group through the Thuringian Forest to the Acillion Cliffs." No other sounds arose, just horses munching on oats as their tails flicked away flies. I lower my voice to a whisper. "Explain yourself."

"Sir, Marius wanted one of us to ensure that you were alright. Lady V has offered multiple rewards for your capture."

"Which is why I came by myself otherwise devoted kinsmen would give me away." I snap. "Did anyone else come too?"

"No, sir. They stayed back at camp."

"At least most of you can follow orders. Go back to Marius and let them know I've been hired."

Kaspar smiled. "Well done! Why can you not return now?"

"Lady V wants to introduce me to Gisela. I'll be back later tonight. Collect supplies for the journey."

"Yes, sir." He readies his horse but before he mounts, turns back towards me. "Will any huntsmen accompany us?" His voice dry and husky.

"I don't know." I reached out to rub his shoulder. Though only a few years younger than me, Kaspar is not without scars. The huntsmen murdered his entire family as he watched from under the floorboards as a young boy. He, like all the wolves, wants revenge. I must remember that I am not the only one wronged by them. While plotting my revenge had nearly consumed my life, others too have valid rationale for joining me to right the wrongs of their past. This journey will test our mettle, and God willing, we come out doing the right thing, otherwise we will be no better than the huntsmen.

I handed him some papers rolled up. "Make sure to leave these in the castle library." About three pages extracted from a book that my grandfather gave me before he passed. I've taken them to every scholar I can locate, and no one can read it. Let's see if Gisela can decipher them. If she can't, I'll know this journey is hopeless. And if she can?

Then I'm one step closer to claiming my crown. Hopefully, she finds the pages before we leave.

\#

I wait in Grandmama's "study." She's made me wait all day and apparently now a few more minutes. She doesn't like to read. Books are like a chair, a chandelier, or a desk. They give gravitas to the owner and set a mood. Or rather, it gives the impression of intelligence. Grandmama has indulged my love of reading, but she doesn't find that it benefits her. Not when she has others to provide the information she wants. Only I haven't been able to provide the knowledge she most desires.

She entered wearing a dressing gown of gold leaf pattern over a royal blue fabric, holding a steaming porcelain cup of coffee. Saying nothing, she sits down to sign some paperwork. I learned long ago to not speak until she did. My cheek was red for a week.

She stopped writing and looked up at me coldly. "I've found dozens of scholars to teach you and where has it gotten me? You can't give me the answers I need. It would have been better to educate someone brighter. You're just not that intelligent, dear."

I ignore the sting of her words.

"I've read every text I could. Are you so sure that Professor Gruden is correct?"

"I am." She continues signing documents. "I did not share every detail from Gruden's analysis last night."

I wait while she takes a sip of coffee. "There are reports that the wise old Owl is returning through the western seas to the Giant Tree above the Acillion Cliffs."

The last one to see my mother alive. I wondered what I would say to him if I ever got the chance.

Many fell to their death attempting to summit through the mountains. It was not a trek for amateurs. "How am I supposed to talk to him? I've never tried to climb to such an elevation."

"I've hired a guide. He and his men will lead you."

"Why? Aren't the huntsmen prepared to take me?"

"They are needed here to protect me. You have three simple tasks. Find the Owl who will help you translate the ancient text. Locate the red diamond and bring it to me. And eliminate Prince Max."

My heart stopped beating for a moment. What did she just ask me to do? Abhorrence and loathing consumed me to be asked to do something so evil. "Why would you ask me to do that?"

"Cadmium will one day be yours and the future queen should lead by example. If you do all three things then the kingdom can never be taken from you."

"If the huntsmen have never found him, maybe he is dead."

"He's alive. I know he is. And his pack of wolves."

"Grandmama, I will do the first two gladly. But I— I cannot kill Prince Max. What if the ancient text states that Max should be King?"

She stood up and walked over to grab my chin. Her nails dig into my skin like daggers. "You will do as I say," she hisses. "Or I will imprison you myself."

Her fingers release me, and I take a step back. I rub at the sting and walk quickly towards the staircase.

"Gisela, I have not dismissed you."

"Yes ma'am." I turned around and stood before her desk waiting for further instructions. Fighting every instinct to return to my library and cry.

"As I said earlier, I've hired a guide." She rings the bell on her desk. "Come in now Rolf."

A man emerged from the hidden door behind the bookcase with mud on his boots and wrinkled clothes. His sleeves are rolled up to his elbows, giving a hint of strong forearm muscles. He looks familiar but I can't place him. The smirk on his face tells me he listened to our conversation. I decided there and then to not trust him. Grandmama beams at him. Another young handsome man for her to collect like her jewels.

He stands adjacent to me and bows to Grandmama. "My lady you're even more radiant in the afternoon."

Well at least this one is intelligent. He figured out her weakness, flattery.

He faces me and bows his head. I noticed the leather wrist cuffs which only warriors wore, his scuffed knee-high boots, and dark molasses-colored whiskers that covered his cheeks and chin.

"I am honored to meet you, Lady Gisela. My men and I will gladly guide you to the Owl and red diamond."

He didn't mention my third task. Without turning my head, I looked past him to Grandmama and she shook her head. Her order to assassinate Prince Max rested on me alone. I won't have the huntsmen. And it remained to be seen if he had overheard our conversation earlier. Perfect. Me, the useless academic, now expected to become an assassin. Rolling my shoulders back, I returned my attention to my guide. "What path shall we take through the Thuringian Forest?"

"The northern route."

"Why not the south? It will take less time, and we will reach Hesperia Mountains in two days."

"Because the northern route has less chance for delays. The southern one may flood, and the dwarves have assembled along that route to mine the selenium.

"We can bribe the dwarves for passage."

He raises an eyebrow. "Have you ever dealt with a dwarf?"

"No."

"A dwarf is only interested in one thing. Wealth through mining. It does not want to be given a gem and then sit home looking at it. If they even smell humans nearby their mines they will attack."

I crossed my arms. "Isn't that why you are there? To protect me?"

I noticed a slight tick at the corner of his jaw. "No, my lady. I was not hired to protect you. Only to guide you. As such I decide which routes we will take in order to get you there safely and return you home."

Even though I'm sure he thinks that he's intimidated me, I won't back down. If I'm going to entrust my life to this man, then I don't see why I shouldn't know more about our journey. "How are we going to find the Owl? And the red diamond?"

"I assumed that your knowledge of ancient Cadmium writing would inform that. Are you not as proficient or intelligent as the people have been led to believe?"

I'm ready to smack the smirk off his face. Who does he think he is? I've had to justify my existence for half my life. Grandmama never said it, but I know she misses my parents. No matter how I've tried I cannot fill the void they left for her. I am the sum of them. My mother's intelligence and my father's skill with archery. But I've never surpassed them.

"My ability to read Cadmium is not in question right now. But your ability to get me to my destination is. No one has found the red diamond in over one hundred years."

He smiled and rolled his shoulders back making him appear taller to me. "I have no doubt we will find it."

"How would *you* even know where to find the Owl?"

"You're just going to have to trust me."

"Trust is earned. It takes more than a handsome face for me to bestow my trust on him."

"Gisela! You will apologize." Grandmama interjects. The wrinkles of annoyance around her mouth fade to a forced smile. "Please forgive Gisela. I can assure she will behave during your journey, or you have my permission to correct her behavior."

I wanted nothing more than to stomp out of the room fuming and indignant. Grandmama had gone too far.

He nodded but a frown and flat eyebrows gave the impression that something upset him. He bows to Grandmama and then to me.

"My men and I were hired as guides not babysitters for spoiled little girls." Pausing a moment before taking one step back. "I will return in two days. Be ready to depart at first morning's light."

He left the room. Just me and a terse Grandmama remain. She waves her hand to dismiss me. I scurried out before she had the chance to change her mind and discipline me.

I spend the rest of the evening reading. Nothing settled my mind. I continually checked the clock. Midnight. One am. Hours had passed since Grandmama gave her edict. I'm still a jumble of emotions. Stunned, annoyed, frustrated, overwhelmed. I considered all the tasks ahead of me. Talk to the Owl. Find the lost red diamond. And lastly, kill Prince Max. I wanted to pull out my hair. Grandmama has lost her mind. I wasn't a killer. I knew how to read ancient texts, but I wasn't close to learning all their secrets. No matter how I scrounge or pat my pillow, nothing soothes my body or mind to find sleep. I'm doomed to toss and turn when all I needed was sleep before the day ahead.

I didn't want to kill anyone. Even if Max's father was rumored to kill my mother. Nothing I did now would bring back my mother. Max was Grandmama's enemy, but did that automatically make him mine?

I hugged myself trying to find some solace in knowing that I couldn't obey this dictate no matter how much I sought her approval.

As I finally drifted off, I thought of Rolf's arrogance and how much more I must endure before I lost my temper. But then in my dream he transformed into my dancing partner from the night before. Remembering his arms around me helped to cut the last tie to consciousness into something resembling the deep sleep of peace.

Chapter 3

What does one pack for a journey to places and landscapes I'd never seen? With men I don't know. I assumed they would protect me, but Rolf had scoffed at the idea that I expected protection. I'm only proficient in archery. Swords are generally too heavy for me to properly wield. Hugo and some huntsmen have tried to teach me self-defense skills but a five-foot, one-inch female against a five-foot, ten-inch male just doesn't possess the same muscle structure.

I suppose I should be grateful we are leaving soon. If I have too long to think about what this journey means to the future and to the past, I will lose my nerve. Grandmama is counting on me. Though I know it is my own expectations that weigh the most.

I have to show Grandmama that I am capable of taking over from her. Duty meant a lot to my father. He devoted his life to his family and country up to his dying breath. I know that duty and responsibility give stability and meaning to life.

"Grandmama is counting on you." My father hugged and kissed me.

"Do you?"

"Of course, little red, but I'm also counting on you to always be your sweet self that does the honorable action."

"What if I don't know what that is?"

"Then you need to pray about it."

Losing both my parents in the same year was heartbreaking. When Mama was murdered Grandmama barely shed a tear, but she didn't leave her room for a week when Papa fell in battle. Mama had just started to teach me how to decipher the old texts. I remember her excitement with about one book she'd found, but then Prince Ansgar murdered her. I wish I knew what book she'd been reading, but it's never been found. When I asked, Grandmama didn't know either. I think picking up mama's hobby was a way to keep her in my life.

I laid out two pairs of hose, a cilice, three camisas, a hairbrush, my quiver and bow, and riding boots. At least they are broken in if we have to walk. Other than that, I've no need for personal supplies. I have the afternoon hours and most of the night to decide what details to copy into a notebook. It is tempting to bring a book or two, but they will only weigh me down. We are traveling by horseback, which means only the essential items are loaded. Rolf already viewed me as frivolous, making others carry my supplies would not improve his opinion.

Scanning through my books, I pay particular attention to information about the Owl and the red diamond.

Nagging on my conscience is Grandmama's private order to me. I could barely contemplate what she asked me to do. To kill was a sin. How could she ask me to do that? What had Prince Max done besides existing as her enemy that warranted killing him?

From the little I knew of Max he is a few years older than me and a brutal warrior. The huntsmen scoff at minstrels who sang of his prowess. But as they had yet to find Max, then he must be intelligent and cunning too. My eyelids drooped, and I shook my head to keep the exhaustion at bay. But the urge to sleep was too great.

I lay there listening to the gentle crackles from the firewood. Closing my eyes with the overwhelming need to pray. *Father, guide my journey. Please help me to make my family proud.* I couldn't continue further. I could never ask God's help to kill a man. Anger flooded my body that Grandmama would dare to even ask me. Max may be my family's enemy. It was rumored that his father killed my parents. But he was still a human being and only God had the right to strike him down. I had every reason to hate the House of Moritz, but I could never seem to summon up that energy. Hate took over every molecule in the body. Killing Max would not bring back my parents.

After waking nearly every hour throughout the night, I am dressed and ready to leave before the sun peaks over the mountain tops. I file away a symbol sheet in my knapsack. Not knowing the distance our journey would take, I packed a floor length red cloak that once belonged to my mother. Red leather piping lining the seams and the layer of insulation makes it weigh about three pounds. I've never worn it but if I can't bring the books then at least I'll have her cloak with me.

When Selene and Lena enter my room, they carry a tray with some papers that curl at the edges.

"A servant found these in the library this morning," Selene informs me. "He thinks it is for you."

I pick up the weathered yet soft parchment. They are from an old text. But which one? The faded symbols are unfamiliar. One suggests a reference to the red diamond's location. I scanned the pages hoping to understand it all.

Glancing at the clock I should be going to meet Rolf, but my gut tells me this is too important to postpone. And I don't think I would be able to fully decipher it without my reference books.

I look at Lena. "Please send word to the guide that I will need a bit more time to prepare."

"What if he wants a more specific time?"

"Just tell him that when he sees me, then I am ready to leave."

Lena smiles and nods. "Very good, Miss."

I scour through the books on my desk. Sitting while I bookmark some pages. I hear Selene ruffle through some drawers. Without looking at her I ask, "What are you doing?"

"If you're going to be busy reading this morning, I should make sure that everything is properly packed for our journey."

My head pops up and I turn. "*Our* journey?"

"Lena and I should go with you. We will help take care of everyone." She fiddles with some clothes and tries to re-fold them.

"Is there something you're not telling me?"

"I worry for Lena and myself without you here." Her voice lowers as she glances toward the door. "Lady V has never looked on either of us favorably. Please let us come."

"Did she say something?"

Selene shook her head but her shifting glances towards the door spoke of worry and fear. I couldn't let anything happen to my two best friends. I would have to watch Grandmama around them when we returned. "Of course you may come with me. I'll think of something to say to Rolf."

I walk over and give her an embrace. "In the meantime, you take care of packing and the bags. I'll see if I can decode these pages before our guide sends someone to collect me. Or heaven forbid he comes himself." My cheeks grow hot at that thought but I ignored it and focused on my task.

#

We'd been waiting for hours, when Gisela *finally* met us in the courtyard, carrying only a knapsack and a fabric bag. At least she is traveling light. I expected her to try bringing her precious books.

"Please saddle two more horses." She ordered the stable master.

I knew it! She has more luggage. Only supply horses don't need saddles...

"Hold on! Who are these horses for?"

"My ladies in waiting, Lady Lena and Lady Selene." She points behind me and waves over two young women. One with midnight black hair and the other with light brown hair. At least they are dressed in pants.

"Absolutely not! We did not pack enough supplies."

"Then you will have to rectify that, won't you?"

"As ladies in waiting, they are not prepared for the journey. Anymore that you are. What skills do they possess that make them needed additions?"

She opens her mouth, but I interject. "Besides companionship for you."

"Both are accomplished horseback riders, they will not slow us down. They also know how to cook and sew. If you have any foresight, you'll see having them will make the journey easier."

I've never met another woman that ignites my temper like this one. "Easier for whom?"

"For us all. Wouldn't your men prefer better food? Their clothes will be in better shape because Lena, and Selene will do the washing."

I groaned and scratched my forehead in frustration. "One woman is hard enough, but three women will elongate our schedule."

"I don't think Lady V gave a deadline."

"The Owl only travels certain times of the year and if we don't make it by January, you will have failed in more than one task."

"They are joining and that is final."

We glared at each other and just as I was about to put my foot down, Marius stepped forward with a smile. "My lady, if you say they are prepared for this excursion, we will believe you."

The corners of her mouth move up. "Thank you." She held out her hand. "And your name is?"

He bowed. "Marius, my lady."

"Thank you, Marius." She turned her head towards me. "It's good to know at least one man here knows how to be a gentleman."

I wanted to give a smart retort to her comment, but Marius intervened once again. "However, as it is two more mouths to feed, would one of your ladies ask the kitchen to provide more rations?"

She nodded and the ladies all went back into the castle. Marius folded his arms, his usual smile now flat. "If that is how you're going to speak to Lady Gisela, you might as well forget the whole plan. You're making an enemy faster than I thought possible."

"What would you suggest? Indulge her every whim."

"Stop acting as if you have no heart. Gisela is innocent of the past. This you know."

His words did give me pause but I'm not ready to admit that he is right.

"Whatever you channeled to get through the ball and dance with her, find it again."

Through clenched teeth. "Fine, then you're in charge of the other two women."

Marius signaled Ludovic and Kaspar over and they discussed who will keep an eye on each woman. It wasn't that I didn't think Gisela, Selene, and Lena were capable of enduring the forest and mountains. Many dangers lay ahead. Too many to name.

Gisela, Selene, and Lena returned with male servants carrying three sacks each for the supply horses. The wolves come forward to help load and secure the cargo to the horses.

"Ladies, let me introduce the men that will assist in this journey." I pointed to each man as I said their name. Marius, my second. The gentlemen are Kaspar, Ludovic, Dominik, Lorenz, and Niko." After introductions I announced. "We will travel through the night and make camp at the base of the mountains."

"Why should we travel through the night? Especially through the mountain passes." Gisela objected.

"There is nowhere to camp once we begin the descent. Every horse and rider will have a lantern. We will be fine."

"I disagree. It is reckless and—"

"You were the one that delayed our departure."

"I apologize for that, but I needed to decipher some papers that I found this morning. I think it will aid in finding the red diamond."

That was good news, but I couldn't let her know that I too was interested in finding that diamond. Or that I would have been overjoyed if she had actually deciphered the papers Kaspar left for her. "Well let's hope making everyone wait over four hours was worth it."

Her eyes squint and nostrils flare. I've probably pushed her too far, but I can't seem to help myself.

"You are being compensated to guide me, and you cannot find the Owl or red diamond without me, so I suggest you change your attitude. Now."

I fight to not roll my eyes. Pushing back on my authority every step of the way. Not literally. Getting through the Forest would take forever if she continued to question all my commands.

"Let's get one thing straight here and now. I am in charge. Lady Vermillion hired me to lead this group, and I will decide what direction, how we will get there, and when we travel." With every word I say I imagine Gisela as a tea kettle about to boil over.

Her cheeks grow from a slight pink to an angry red. Now I know why Marius teases me so often. It's fun to poke someone's temper, especially when you know that you have the ability to make it erupt.

"If we find the red diamond because of some papers that you just read, when as a lady of leisure, you've supposedly had all the time in the world. Then I will defer to you. Not before." I take one step and lean down so I stare into her hazel eyes. "Do you understand me?"

She folds her arms over her chest and her lips barely move to hiss, "yes."

Gisela is a little spitfire. The red hair is a complete tell-tale sign of that. But she doesn't seem to wield her temper to only get her way.

It was midafternoon when we mounted up to leave. Nearly an entire day wasted! My temples pound as if a blacksmith is shaping a blade on an anvil inside my head. This journey was a long time coming and it seems the outcome will be delayed even further if Gisela has anything to say about it. Yet I feel hopeful for the first time in a while. If she read those pages, then she has brought her grandmama's downfall one step closer.

\#

I watched as the caravan with Gisela and Rolf set out away from the castle, until the sun set behind the mountains and purple dusk made the path faint. My fingers curled over the wooden balcony railing, and I breathed deep yet the tension between my shoulder blades would not ease. Gisela will fail me. Of that, I'm sure. Not that she will mean to. She is too much like her parents. They valued honor more than anything else. Honor did not ensure power.

"The huntsmen are assembled and ready to follow Gisela and the ruffian group my lady."

Hugo, the lead huntsman, announces behind me. He knew I'd be sending him before I called. Gisela will never be the queen I've been or rather will be once I used her to find the red diamond. And then Rolf. I can't decide what puts me on edge about him. He appears hungry for something. And he reminds me of someone, but I couldn't remember who. His gray eyes haunt me like a nightmare.

Hugo clears his throat, reminding me of his presence. I sashayed past him. Hoping my perfume of foxglove catches his attention. The huntsmen have been my allies for over twenty years. Without them I would not be where I am. Akin to a queen. Yet I am not a queen. And I'm tired of waiting for them to find Prince Max. He is the last of the Moritz lineage and the one standing in my way to a legitimate throne.

"Follow them. Don't let anyone know you're there."

"Any other instructions, my lady?"

"Keep one of the ravens so you can update me, when you reach an agreement with the dwarves how to dispose of her."

He nods. Near the balcony window are two small crystal glasses on a small wooden table. The decanter close by holds special brandy that I've spent decades perfecting. Only one barrel is made each year and only for my consumption.

I know Hugo watches my every movement. His longing gaze pleads that I'll offer him a glass. Which I will never do. "Do you expect Gisela to find and kill Prince Max?"

I nearly spit out the sip that I relished on my tastebuds. "Not at all! I want her to think she will. But I know she doesn't possess the strength to actually assassinate him."

"She'll be lucky to even locate him."

I nod. Yet I know Gisela wants my approval more than anything. If I dangle the right motivation she may loosen her moral code. But that is what I do best. Locating someone's weakness and motivating them with it. For my own benefit.

"Are you afraid of what she may learn from the Owl?" His voice hushes even though it is only the two of us on the balcony.

"No." Hugo as he aged tended to worry about his past misdeeds and wanted to atone for them. It was becoming a liability. Something perhaps to be taken care of soon. "Even if the Owl shares your secret there is nothing Gisela can do about it. She cannot turn back time."

"I don't know what to do if she asks me about it."

"She's a sentimental fool."

"She's your granddaughter," he snaps. "Maybe you should explain more about your choices from long ago. She may understand…"

Eager to be done talking about this subject I shook my head and walked back into the room towards the door to my private chamber. "You have your orders. Don't disappoint me." I close the door and make my way to my dressing room.

Sitting down at my dressing table my reflection is the only thing that's changed in ten years. The wrinkles are new but the white hair, red lips, and an angled sculpted face remain constant. Much as I should relax now that Gisela has finally set out, I am still annoyed with him.

I used to share every thought, but Hugo is not the huntsman he used to be. Max is rumored to be one of the finest warriors. Gisela is no match for Max. I can spin her death, ensuring that those who have hidden him for years will no longer protect him. Gisela will die for a noble cause, like her mother.

Chapter 4

I stopped the caravan after we'd traveled nearly twenty-four hours on the edge of Thuringian Forest. None of the women complained. Though Marius glared the last few hours, which needed no translation. I pushed them too hard, but I wanted and needed to know what they were capable of enduring.

"Men, build a fire and unload food for supper. Ladies, if you would please prepare the meal? My men will see to your horses."

"Thank you, but I think we should see to our own horses." Gisela countered as she dismounted before Dominik could assist her.

I decided to let her have her way this time and nodded. Marius helped Selene down and Ludovic assisted Lena. I supervised the other wolves as they collected firewood, set up tents, and ensured that each horse had enough to eat. As we are about to enter the forest our survival balanced upon the health of our horses. We all finished our tasks and sat down around the fire as the ladies handed out portions of cheese, bread, and some chicken for everyone. Everyone was quiet as they devoured their meals.

The ladies say goodnight and head to their tent. My eyes followed Gisela as she walked back to her tent. Kaspar volunteered for the first watch and the others chose their watch time. I would take the last watch beginning at four am. I began my walk to check the perimeter. Should anyone find the camp we are out in the open but close enough to run into the thick dark forest. But it's what hiding in the forest that chills my blood.

"Should I tell the others to not expect to sleep every other night?" Marius joined me.

I dramatically sighed, but I knew Marius' intentions were good. "I won't have us travel all night again unless we absolutely must. Does that satisfy you?"

He rolled his eyes. I accepted his criticisms, but it still annoyed me that he questioned me. I had to take a few calming breaths. He is my best friend, and he has devoted his life to my family's cause at the detriment to his own family. As the leader of the Wolves, I relied on my second's feedback. Marius reminded me to be a human and act humanely. The flaws and shortcomings that come with being a human waste time. Emotions crippled humans. Responsibilities and duties were easier for me to understand. If I allowed my emotions to control me then Lady V won a long time ago.

Marius waved his hand in my face. I blinked and return to our conversation. He smirked and rested his left hand on the hilt of the sword at his hip. "We have a long way to go, and it makes no sense to exhaust everyone."

"Understood." I nodded and walked just past him, when turned my head to whisper under my breath, 'thank you.' We turned to head to camp.

Marius nudged me with his elbow. "What do you know about Lady Selene?"

I stopped and Marius nearly stumbled into me. "Nothing. Gisela never brought up before this morning that she was bringing her two ladies in waiting. She's comely but do not plan to woo her." I crossed my arms and say with the utmost dictatorial voice, "We have dozens of dangers that await us. I forbid you and the other wolves from creating any new dangers."

Marius raised his eyebrows. "When is flirting with a woman a danger?"

"It is when nothing can come of it."

"Why can nothing come of it? We know nothing about Selene. Perhaps she secretly does not support Lady V."

"Whether she does or not, doesn't matter. We are responsible for their welfare and that's it." I stepped forward and jabbed my finger into his chest. "Stay committed to the task at hand. We cannot afford to miss this opportunity. No matter how tempting it is to ponder a life with a good woman and a home."

"One day that may be so. You can't ignore that Gisela is a comely lady." His usual calm to my bluster diffuses me.

"Until I've brought Lady V and the huntsmen down I—we cannot be distracted."

"You have feelings for Gisela." His grin spread across his whole face.

Drat. If I denied it too vehemently than Marius would tease me incessantly. "No." My denial is weak.

"We all saw you watching her."

"That means nothing."

"That red hair is..." He leaves his last word hanging as if waiting for me to reveal my feelings by readily agreeing or denying.

"Goodnight." I marched off not waiting for him.

He hollered at me, "Pleasant dreams. Rolf!"

Utter nonsense. Attracted to Gisela? She is the means to getting back my crown. Marius does have a point that Gisela and I cannot spar every time we speak to each other. We already have many odds stacked against us, and I shouldn't make an enemy of Gisela. Eventually she will learn my real identity and hate me. But until the I needed her help.

\#

Selene, Lena, and I all fell asleep the moment we laid down. Traveling down the mountain pass at night was terrifying but like Rolf had told me the lantern did help as well as the gentle lullaby the men sang. I overheard Lena ask why they sang, and Ludovic told her that it soothed the horses.

The howl of a wolf woke me, and I shivered. I had a choice to either curl under my blanket again or warm myself by the fire. The warmth and comfort of a fire in the middle of the night won over my fatigue. I had no idea of the time or who was on watch duty. *Please let it be anyone but Rolf.* Tiptoeing out of the tent I saw a figure sitting on a log by the fire looking down. The closer I got my heart knew it was Rolf. My heart beat jumped into my throat. I didn't think he'd heard me, but I couldn't retreat now. Feeling a bit shy but wanting to continue the front of prickliness, I continued forward. One of my steps alerted him to my presence and he jumped up pulling his sword from his scabbard, ready to fight the intruder.

I held my hands up. "It's just me."

He exhaled. "What are you doing awake? You should be asleep."

"Don't you need sleep?"

"Not unless I have to." He quipped. "I slept before I relieved Dominik from guard duty." He looked around. Though I couldn't imagine what he'd see when the sky was still pitch black. "I am responsible for you, your ladies, and my men. The choices I make have consequences for everyone."

I tried to make my comment lighthearted. "Yes, like depriving us of sleep."

"You and the ladies made it didn't you? And without any complaint." His tone softened. "I was proud of you all."

Even though Rolf aggravated me, he was trying to get us all there swiftly. He was just doing his job. If I was to accomplish anything I needed him. It would do me no good to alienate him. "I'm sorry I delayed us."

"You already explained. But I appreciate your apology."

We sat in silence for a few minutes. Eager to continue our quiet truce I thought of something else to say. "Do you want to know what the pages said?"

"Of course."

"They showed up in the library. Selene and Lena brought them to me just as I was ready to go downstairs. Some of the symbols were familiar but others I'd never seen before." The excitement of the discovery coursing through my veins. But for the first time I was telling someone whom I hoped shared my similar excitement for learning about our history. Not for the hidden riches to be found.

"They discussed the origins of the red diamond. How a young orphan girl was lost on the Acillion Cliffs after the dragon queen attacked her family believing they stole her eggs. When she had the little girl in her talons ready to eat her, the little girl pleaded with her to kill her soon so she could be with her family. The dragon queen was struck by the little girl's plea. She had made the little girl an orphan and now she had no children of her own, so she offered to raise the little girl as her own."

Rolf's features seem captivated by my story. "This is quite a story."

"Oh, it gets better! The little girl takes a chance and grows to love the dragon like her own mother. She confesses to the dragon that she and her family had eaten her eggs because they'd been starving. The dragon queen was terribly upset but eventually forgave the little girl, making her promise to always tell her the truth. As the little girl grew up to a beautiful woman she fell in love with a handsome lord. As he knew the dragon queen claimed a human woman as her daughter, he hoped that he would inherit all the wealth the dragon queen possessed. So, he tricked her into marrying him and he made her tell him where the dragon queen kept all her gold. Following the lord the dragon's cave, she comes across them fighting and when he tells the dragon queen that it was her daughter who told him where to find the gold, the dragon stumbles, and the lord thrusts his sword close to the dragon's heart.

The daughter rushes in and stands in front of the dragon before the lord can make the deathblow. She sobs 'forgive me mother. He tricked me. I deserve death for being a fool.' The dragon queen, grateful for her daughter telling her the truth, crushes the lord with her tail. Before she dies, she tells her daughter she loves her and to take care of the kingdom. She vanished, leaving behind the red diamond, which the daughter told everyone was the heart of the dragon queen for her people."

"So that little girl is Bellona the First?"

"Yes." I smiled. "Do you know the history of Cadmium, well?"

"Just the basics."

"I wonder why that story was forgotten?"

"It's fairly unbelievable."

My head jerked towards him and tilted wanting to hear his explanation before I got defensive. "Are you saying I made up the story?"

"No! I believe you. It's just that dragons have been extinct for hundreds of years and you're telling me that a dragon queen raised the woman that founded this kingdom. Like I said, it's a lot to take in."

"That's true."

"Did the papers talk about the red diamonds' whereabouts?"

"Not exactly. It gave clues as to where it had been kept but I've never heard about a castle close to Jormagne Forest. Have you?"

He stared into the fire. "I've never seen a castle there." He inhaled and faced me with a half-smile. "But sounds like that will be added to our journey after we find the Owl." Lowering his eyebrows he said in a sarcastic yet serious tone, "You'll be sure to tell me if there are any other destinations we need to add, right?"

"I promise." I smiled keeping my lips pressed together.

He laughed, and I suddenly hoped I would have the chance to make him laugh more often. "As long as I have your promise on that. What are you hoping to learn from the owl?"

Before I can answer we are interrupted when Lena walked out of the tent, her head turning right and left looking for something just as the early morning sky is shifting from pitch black to shadowy blue. "Is Selene with you?"

"No, she was asleep in the tent, when I came out here." I glanced at Rolf.

"Are you sure she wasn't there?" He stood and grabbed a burning torch.

As he purposefully walked towards the tent he whistled a shrill alert. The rest of the tent flaps opened, and the men rushed out. Rolf pointed right, left, and behind the tent. "Move slow and check for footprints."

They spread out searching behind the tents and the areas surrounding the camp.

Lena and I stood watching not sure what we needed to do. Rolf hadn't given us an assignment.

She turned to me, "Before you left the tent did you see her inside?"

I shook my head, worry nagging at me. Selene wouldn't just wander off. Another whistle pierced the air. We ran to the location of its origin.

The men stand in a semi-circle about twenty yards from the back of my tent.

"What did you find?" I asked breathlessly.

Rolf pointed to footprints that lead towards the forest. "There is a mixture of sizes."

I inspected the ground and saw some prints smaller than my foot size and others about a normal male size. Too scared to voice Selene's words from the other day about Grandmama, I faced Rolf. "What do you think happened?"

He remained silent. Studying the ground and the glancing up to look around the perimeter. "I'm sure some of these are dwarf prints. Others are men." He folded his arms, but now is attention focused on me. "The question is why? Why would men and dwarves want with Selene? Did they even kidnap the right woman?"

Lena spoke up before I can stop her. "Lady V has never liked Selene and I. We worried that she would do something to us if we didn't accompany Gisela."

"Why would Lady V want you gone?" Ludovic inquired as all the men joined us.

Lena stared at the ground, her chin nearly touching her chest. "She wanted us to report back to her about Gisela."

Struck but not surprised that Grandmama would try to use my friends to spy on me, I wrapped one arm around her waist. "I believe you, Lena." As I turned my head to address Rolf. "Selene did ask for her and Lena to join me, worried that Grandmama would have the huntsmen do something to them while I was away."

"I still find it difficult to believe that Lady V would order someone kidnapped for disobeying her," Ludovic asserted.

"She's done much more for less." I'm hoarse and numb worrying over my friend and angry that I didn't take Selene seriously before. "We must go after her!"

Rolf shook his head. "With the number of prints, they would overwhelm us if the group followed them. They would expect that."

"Then what do you suggest?" I'm prepared to argue with Rolf on this. I wouldn't leave my best friend to suffer whatever horrible fate awaited her.

Marius stepped forward. "I will follow them and bring back Selene, alone."

Rolf nodded and Marius raced to his tent.

I watched their quick interaction. Grateful that Marius spoke up, but Rolf couldn't mean to send only one man, by himself! "Please Rolf, he can't go alone! I know there are many but one man going alone is suicide. Send another of your men. Two men can sneak in just as easily as one."

He walked back towards the fire and began cleaning up. "I've made my decision, Gisela. Have faith that Marius will save her."

"But—"

His turned back towards me, eyes and face flashed in anger. "Leave it be!"

I closed my mouth embarrassed to be yelled at in front of everyone.

He addresses his men. "Everyone eat some breakfast, then break down camp and pack up supplies. We leave in an hour."

Marius ran out of his tent, carried his gear to his horse and grabbed the reins of Selene's horse to secure them to the pommel of his saddle.

"Meet us at the base of Scarnigian Pass." Rolf yelled out as Marius climbed into his saddle and galloped away.

Please dear God let him bring Selene back to us. Lena steered me towards our tent. One lone tear rolled down my cheek. With so many eyes watching I can't break down now. Nor would I allow myself.

#

The rest of the day is spent on guard as we traveled into the heart of the Thuringian Forest.

Everyone including Rolf is pensive and focused. I'm sure they are concerned for Marius and Selene but something else weighs on them. I decided to not ask and just do as I'm told.

We reached a river about late afternoon that looks safe enough to cross but the sunlight dwindles with each passing moment.

Rolf held up his fist. He instructed Ludovic and Dominik to set up camp in the nearby grove of apple trees that surrounds us.

Well at least we will have something else for dinner tonight besides bread and cheese.

After supper Rolf and I found ourselves alone on opposite sides of the fire. Everyone else is asleep in their tents. Above the apple trees the evergreen giant trees blocked all views of the night sky. More than the trees watched us I knew, but in the middle of the night when sleep is not a restful place, conversation with anyone is the most welcome option, rather than lying in bed with only worrisome thoughts.

At least it should have been. Strands of Rolf's hair fell on his forehead and his eyebrows hovered closely over his eyes. His expression so focused. So angry. A little notch of skin swells between his eyebrows as he glared into the fire. And his jaw is clenched so hard he might have a headache in the morning. I'll admit I'm a little worried. Maybe he's angry with me for disagreeing with him this morning. But so far, he hasn't said anything that indicated that. Since he hasn't made a gesture to speak all I can do is ask. "Do you want to share your troubles?"

He blinked and peered through the fire at me as if he's remembering that I am still sitting here. Releasing a deep breath, he stood and walked over to stand before me. Looking into his eyes I see something resembling weariness and sadness. "We will talk tomorrow night. Get some rest we have another long day ahead of us." And he walked to his tent and I called out, "Goodnight!"

I'm a bit disappointed but I also cannot make him talk to me. Is he sad about Marius and Selene? I don't know anything about his family or Rolf, the man. No one intrigues me like he does. Much less the jumble of emotions he elicits is disconcerting. I can only hope I'll find surer footing with him as we continue on this journey.

Chapter 5

I woke up with the plan to apologize to Gisela for being brusque last night. Also to assure her that Marius will save Selene. I'm not sure of much right now but I'm confident in that.

The wolves and Lena are assembled by the burning embers of the fire. Gisela must still be sleeping or getting ready. Lena stood by the fire and rubbed her hands together over the flames. She still shivered while Ludovic handed her a cloak lined with fox fur. Autumn is ebbing into winter. The red, orange, and yellow leaves are beginning to fall while the green evergreens are just as they are in summer. We will encounter snow before too long. I finished my eating an apple and tighten the belt on Deimhain's saddle.

Where was Gisela? So much for her wanting to cooperate. "Lena, tell Gisela it is time to leave."

"She left this morning to go to the river. She told me she would tell you."

Curse that woman! What could she possibly be doing running off without telling me?

I leapt into the saddle "Stay here!"

My heels nudge Deimhan's flanks and we ran towards the river. I hoped to quickly locate the errant Little Miss Know-It-All before too much time was lost.

Minutes fly by and my thoughts sank into worry. Before too long I'm frantic to find her, not knowing if more dwarves are out there looking for slave labor and kidnapped her too. I also hadn't told Gisela that in one of footprints an H was visible. The huntsmen were following us. Either Lady V didn't trust me or Gisela.

Following the riverbank I didn't see any footprints of humans, only animals like badgers, beavers, and deer. Finally, I spotted a flash of red cloak in a meadow picking the last of the wildflowers. Relief that she's unharmed gave way to anger that I'd never unleashed before. "Has time spent in the library reading books erased all your sense of safety?"

Her unbound auburn hair whipped around as she jumped up. I dropped from the saddle and grabbed her shoulders. "You run off the morning after your best friend is kidnapped! What if they were looking for you too? What were you thinking?"

Shock, confusion, and apprehension mixed in her eyes. "I'm sorry! I thought I would collect some flowers and herbs to brew some teas before they're all gone in winter."

I expected bluster from her. Not an actual apology. "Lena said you were going to tell me where you were going. Why didn't you?"

She looked away and her voice catches. "I didn't want to make a nuisance of myself."

Dumbstruck I remember how Lady V spoke to about her to me. "Gisela is not very bright." It wouldn't take much to eventually break down someone's self-confidence if that is how her grandmother always spoke about her. Comments like that would eventually find the source and eventually draw blood. I crooked my finger under her chin and gently pulled her gaze up to meet mine. "You are not a nuisance."

She said nothing. Though I noticed the moisture that gathered at the corners of her eyes. I pity her and what she has endured so far as Lady V's granddaughter. But my pity cannot distract me. I released her chin and stepped back.

A voice from the branches above us made us both jump. "The Owl is waiting for you." I pushed Gisela behind me I searched the branches. I only spotted a red winged blackbird.

He flew down to my eye level and bobbed his tiny head to the left. "Follow me."

And flew northward toward the Minacious Peak. One place that I never wanted to go. But now I didn't have a choice. That is if the blackbird spoke the truth otherwise he was leading us into a trap.

"Where is your bow?"

She pointed to a pomegranate tree ahead. Hanging from a branch is her quiver and bow. She collected that while I check that I've got my sword, crossbow, and a few daggers. I helped Gisela onto Deimhen and climbed up behind her. Following the blackbird, I wished there were a way to send word to the wolves where we were going but we cannot lose this chance to talk with the Owl.

The closer we come to the opening of cave at the base of the peak, the less sunlight finds peaked through the overgrowth of brambles and bushes of thorns. Deimhein swishes his tail repeatedly and Gisela gripped his mane so tightly her knuckles turned white.

I pulled one dagger from my belt and slide it into her boot. She turned and looked at me. Her raised eyebrows signaled that she wanted an explanation. "Just in case. And I do mean a last resort."

The blackbird hovered above the opening to the cave. We dismounted, and I left the reins over Deimhein's neck so he could escape if necessary. We stood at the black yawning entrance. The dank damp smell chilled me to the bone. Gisela gripped my arm as she leaned against. Her breathing matched pace with mine. If we meet the Owl, I can only hope to find answers to questions I've waited most of my life to ask.

The blackbird landed on a ledge above the entrance . "The Owl will see only see one of you at a time."

"No, he will see us together!" I insisted as blasts of wind and sounds of rumbling traveled closer from inside the cave. A mass of blackbirds flew at us as Gisela and I dove for the ground. When we looked up a fox sat perfectly poised before us.

He looked down his long snout at us. "The Owl will see you first...Rolf."

I almost forgot how to breath. The way the fox paused before saying my 'fake' name, gave me chills. But how could he know?

I shook my head. "I cannot leave her unprotected."

Gisela placed her hand on my bicep. Her expression wary yet calm, that I didn't expect from her.

"Go. I'll be fine. I'm sure the Owl didn't bring us here only to harm us."

The blackbird's little head nodded up and down. The fox also concurred. "Oh no indeed the Owl is most anxious to talk with you both."

"Yell out if you need me." I took one last look at Gisela set off down the ominous dark passageway trying to be prepared for anything that came at me. I dodged cobwebs and overwhelming stench of sulfur infiltrated my nostrils. A distant tiny light many yards away is my only guide. Each step I took I waited for something to fall or to jump out at me. I used one hand on the rock as a guide and the other held my sword before me. The light grew larger the closer I got to a boulder that left only a sliver of a doorway to squeeze through.

Once I made it through, my eyes had to adjust to the abundance of light. I blinked several times but it was no mirage in front of me. A full library that rivaled one from a university. Four stories tall with rows of leather-bound volumes. Three shelves for each level with ivy ladders, not wood. Gisela would never want to leave this room.

Books were a luxury and not something that I could keep while living as a vagabond, but I remembered how I spent many hours with my father and tutors in the castle library. One of the many things Lady V stole from me.

I searched the room. Nothing moved nor seemed out of place. An owl in a library would be inconspicuous enough. The grandfather clock gonged, and I whirled around with my sword ready. In the corner, an old man sits in large upholstered high-back chair with a leather egg shaped top. His white beard reached the middle of his chest. I lowered my sword as he eyed me over his spectacles. He took them off and blew on the lenses. Then polished them with a handkerchief.

Who is this man? Could *he* be the Owl?

The corners of his lips turn up and smirking, he eyed me again. "Yes, Your Highness. It is I."

The Owl *is* a man! How did no one know that?

"Many people once knew me, Max. Now, I am only spoken about in whispers. Like a superstition."

"How did you know who I am?"

Closing the book on his lap, he traced the edges with his fingers. "The more important question is what do you seek here?"

"I want to avenge my family. I want my kingdom back."

"You heart and mind have only focused on that. But God gave you a will. Wrong was done to your family. But is God using you to right that wrong?"

Never once had I considered God directing my choices. My grandfather and father ruled wisely. They did not deserve to suffer the deaths they endured. I opened my mouth to protest.

"Don't be so quick to answer. Hate has ruled your heart. How can any decision be wisely made when no reflection or prayer was ever attempted?"

"How can prayer help? God does not answer selfish prayers." I know it's spiteful to say but I'm overcome with burning acid in my throat if the Owl doesn't support my crusade.

The Owl nodded but his frown spoke of sadness. "God has asked much of you. But you must take heart. He wouldn't ask if he didn't know what remarkable things you are capable of achieving."

"Then why has God made me wait this long?"

"That is only for God to know." He stood nearly a foot shorter than me. His frail frame leaned on a gnarled oak cane. Crooking his finger at me, he shuffled one foot after another towards a table where a large book lay open.

The House of Moritz genealogical tree unfolds before me. My parents and grandparents names and dates remind me of the legacy I am fighting to reclaim. As the last of the Moritz line, I was left alive for a purpose. *Wasn't I?* Running my fingers over the pages and their names, the ache of missing them threatened to overwhelm me. At this moment if the Owl had an answer I would make any vow, oath, or promise I could with God to avenge them.

Clearing his throat the Owl turned the weathered pages to the Vermillion family tree. My glance landed on Gisela's name.

"You have fought every day of your life for revenge. But I wonder what you will do when revenge is complete. What do you want for yourself?"

I looked away not willing to consider the endless possibilities of next steps when I defeated Lady V.

The Owl's hushed tone penetrated through my stubbornness. "Until you are ready to consider that I don't think you'll find the conclusion you're hoping for."

He sighed and hobbled back into his chair. As if the few steps weathered him, his voice came out with soft pants. "I'll be watching you and Gisela. Only together…" He ceased speaking still catching his breath. A barn owl swooped down and landed on the high-backed chair and began to coo a lullaby.

Up above at the top level of the library is a skylight made of clear, green, and cobalt glass. My mind can't make out how there is skylight in this cave of solid rock below a mountain. Snowy, burrowing, Eurasian, Ural, tawny, long eared, and Great Horned owls all perched at different spots. My usual situational awareness failed to notice their presence.

A snore rumbled out from the Owl. The cooing barn owl pointed his wing towards another door. "Leave through there. Once the Owl speaks with Gisela, she will meet you."

Bereft that I'm not going to get a chance to ask more questions, I exited. While I waited, I'll have to think through the next steps of our journey. That is preferable than dwelling on what the Owl said about my life choices and how Gisela now fits into it.

\#

Waiting for Rolf, I sat on the stone floor. Wrapping my arms around my knees to ward off the cold, I rested my head on them hoping to rest the fear that gnawed at me.

The fox edged closer to me and rested against my side offering comfort and warmth. Petting his thick fur soothed my nerves. "Thank you."

His purring vibrated through my fingers all the way to my bones.

The blackbird fluttered over me and perched on one knee. "Why do you want to see the Owl?"

"He was the last one to see my mother alive. Maybe he knows something about how and why she died."

He tilted his head almost touching the top of his wing. "You seem unsure about that Miss."

"About what?"

He ignored my question to ask his own. "Who told you how she died?"

"My grandmother."

"Does your grandmother ever lie?"

My heart wanted to shout yes, but I was not prepared to dishonor my only living family member.

"You know in your heart the truth even if you're not ready to acknowledge it." He spread his wings and flew up a few feet. "The Owl will see you now."

I followed him through the rock hallway. My heartbeat raced wondering what awaited me. Will the Owl have the answers to my questions? Would I finally learn the truth about my mother's death? We entered a library that I'd only dreamt of in my favorite daydreams. Four levels of leather-bound volumes contained more knowledge than I can ever pray to possess. I wanted to pore through every volume drinking in the knowledge from every page like a someone lost in the desert who found fresh water.

The blackbird gestured to the two chairs in front of the fire. "Please sit down. The Owl will be in shortly." He flew out the same way we entered.

Not being able to help myself I made my way over to the closest bookshelf and scanned through the titles. History, geography, philosophy, animal references, and sword manuals. The would interest Rolf. I grabbed the red leather-bound book and flicked through a few pages, especially the illustrations.

"I would not have predicted you'd choose that volume to read. At least not the first."

I jumped and searched for the source. An old man with a long white beard stood a few yards away. My head swiveled back and forth looking for the way he entered. Seeing none, I snapped the book shut and put it back onto the shelf.

I moved closer and the old man held out his hand while leaning on his cane. He smiled and I put my hand in his.

"Your mother would be so proud of you, Gisela."

I blinked back a tear as my throat ached. "I would hope so, Sir."

"Come sit. Rolf can wait for you a bit longer." We settled into the chairs by the fire.

"Why do they call you the Owl?"

He laughed a bit louder, making me think he enjoy the irony. "A name is just a name. It is the stories that matter. I haven't lived among men in eons. Does it matter how truth transcends?"

"Yes, truth matters. Truth is real."

"So is faith. And you know it is not always tangible."

"Faith is harder to understand as I age." I'd only found comfort in reading, archery, and time with Selene and Lena. I hadn't prayed since my parents died. Grandmama didn't insist on prayer.

He made a tisking sound. "Your mother was a scholar like you, but she knew faith superseded any quest for knowledge she could achieve."

"Please, sir. How did she die? Grandmama told me you were the last one to see her alive."

"Did she tell you that I was man?"

"No. She never told me much about you."

"So then how would she know that I was the last one to see her alive?"

Like a punch to my gut, I exhaled harshly and laced my fingers in my lap squeezing them back and forth. Thoughts that swirled in my head for years but never surfaced are now fresh nightmares. For how long had Grandmama lied to me? Was anything I knew about my mother's death real? I took deep breaths, attempting to steady myself.

"You will need that inner strength in the days ahead."

"I'm afraid that it will break me...accepting the truth of the past."

"Your mother worried about that too. As did your father. But God will be with you."

I sniffed, not wanting to break down in front of him. "I haven't prayed in the longest time. Will he listen to me now?"

"God will always listen and help you. Though, it just may not be the help you are specifically asking for."

"The tasks my grandmama gave me. I don't know what to do. I've found you. Or rather you found me. She wants me to kill Prince Max. I can't kill anyone. What should I do?"

"Pray, my dear. Only there will you find the answers."

I wished I could find somewhere quiet to cry and collect my thoughts.

The Owl's hand rests on mine, and he squeezed it. "Remember, you won't be alone. A warrior was sent for you, but you'll have to trust him."

My heart skipped a beat. Someone who fought for me. Not to use me for their own benefit. Could it be Rolf? I was afraid that he would only ever see me as a spoiled brat. And I wanted him, more than anyone else, to know me. Beyond the love of books. But would he see a woman worth loving and respecting?

The Owl pointed towards another door, his voice difficult to hear and growing raspy. "Rolf is waiting beyond that door for you. May God be with you both on your journey."

Did he just dismiss me? "Oh, please, sir. I have more questions especially about my mother."

"You will find your answers soon enough." The Owl settled his head against the chair and closed his eyes.

Did I fail once more by not pushing for the outcome I wanted? Hopefully, Rolf got more information. My feet are heavy like rocks as I exited the room. Wistfully and with regret I think how leaving the Owl and his library is one of the hardest things I've ever done.

Chapter 6

I blink adjusting my eyes to the daylight outside. Rolf stands other with his back to the cave. Just looking up at the sky. I want to ask him about his conversation. And I'm equally eager to share about mine. He doesn't turn around right away. For someone who is always on guard I wonder if something is wrong. I wait just to watch him. I take one step closer and leaves crackle underneath my step. He whirls, his sword ready.

He looks at me as if he's seeing me for the first time. What did the Owl tell him? From the moment I met him I noticed his tall, muscled build, greyish blue eyes, and masculine facial features. But now I too see him with fresh eyes. Could he be the warrior that the Owl spoke of? While every lonely girl dreams of a man who will care, love, and protect her. I always wanted those things, but as a woman I want more. I want a connection, a promise made to God and each other that we love, honor, and cherish one another through all of life's trials.

What am I talking about? Rolf and I have no such understanding. How can I be sure this is not just a passing infatuation? Because I've never allowed myself to dream about a husband. Grandmama wanted all male attention on her. Thus, why I've never spent much time with any man. I didn't want to know if I'd always come in second place. It was easier to hide in the library and not try to compete. If Grandmama viewed me as a competitor for fairest in the land, I shudder to think how she would treat me.

And most important of all, Rolf's never spoken anything beyond his hired task of leading me to the red diamond. He's never given me a sign that I am anything more than a task to him.

We stand opposite one another just taking in the presence of the other. Leaves fall from the trees like rainfall. Both of us are changed by our conversations, yet neither can formulate the words to express that.

His voice comes out hoarsely. "The others will wonder where we are." He places his middle finger and thumb on the edge of his mouth. A shrill whistle slices the crisp air.

His horse finds us within ten minutes. I climb into the saddle and Rolf behind me. I try to maintain some distance, my posture stiff. Yet his arms encase my body, and every nerve ending is sensitive to his presence.

We reach camp and his men hurry to meet us.

"Where have you been?"

"What happened?

Lena rushes to hug me. I thread my arm through hers and guided her to our tent to talk privately.

"Ladies we leave in an hour." Rolf calls. "We must reach the Acillion Cliffs by tomorrow."

Lena whispers. "Do you think Marius will be there with Selene?"

"We can only hope and pray."

As we enter our tent, Lena grabs my arms. "Why did you run off this morning? Why did you tell me that you would tell Rolf?" Her voice catches and I could hear the tears in her voice before they even fell from her eyes. "Selene was kidnapped, and I was petrified something happened to you. Please don't do that to me!"

"I'm sorry. I was wrong." I hug her again, hoping she knows I didn't run off on purpose.

She wipes at the tears and clears her throat. "I've never known you to lie. Why?"

I turned and busied myself with folding my clothes into my knapsack. "I needed to take a walk and think through some things. Pick some wildflowers."

"You know going anywhere by yourself is dangerous. It's not like you to take risks like that. What did you need to think through?"

I must have really scared Lena for her to become a stern nursemaid.

I turn and notice both fists are anchored on her hips. Her lips and eyebrows both flat lines showing her displeasure with me.

I can't help but smirk. "I remember someone giving our tutor fits when we were little girls because you would wander off. When we return to the Scarlet Palace will you be apologizing to Madame Belmont?"

Her frown cracks but she tries to maintain her no-nonsense stance. "Madame always knew where to find me."

"The stables, but she didn't know you only went so you could watch Sir Darius on the training grounds."

"Not until you shared that information with her."

"She wouldn't have hesitated to make up a worse story to tell Grandmama."

"You've always protected us." She takes a deep breath. "Will you please tell me why you left by yourself?"

How could I explain the mess I felt inside? That I wanted to experience falling in love. For so long I studied, hoping to find answers in books. I wasn't going to get back my mother and father from books. I don't know what caused this awakening for life.

As much as I struggled with the feelings Rolf elicited, I couldn't stay away from him. I couldn't admit to Lena much less myself, that I wanted him to think well of me.

No one questioned me like he did. Questioned my opinions, my intentions. Equally infuriating and refreshing. He made me think and see things that I never thought of before.

He saw me as a spoiled child. Why did I care what he thought of me? It rankled because how could I prove to him that I was trying to be a strong and wise woman? I made a mistake this morning by running off. Yet maybe if I hadn't, then we wouldn't have met the Owl? I would have to be patient and wait for tonight when we could chat by the fire alone.

"I promise to not venture off by myself again." I hoped that would satisfy Lena because I wasn't ready to discuss my inner turmoil yet.

With our packs ready we met the men outside and mounted our horses. Throughout our ride I relished the views and seeing part of the kingdom I'd only read about. At one point there was a grand castle sat on the Acillion Cliffs. As much as I hoped that Marius and Selene would be there waiting for us, maybe if we must wait for them there will be time to explore the cliffs and perhaps find remnants of the castle.

I nudge my horse to catch up to Rolf. He glances at me, his light brown eyebrows raised, waiting for me to speak.

"Will we be traveling through the night to reach the cliffs?"

He shakes his head. "We should reach them by nightfall."

Nothing more is said for a few minutes. I should probably fall back to rejoin Lena, but Rolf doesn't show that he is annoyed with my presence. I'd like to ask him to discuss the events earlier today, but a gut feeling tells me to wait for him to mention that topic. "Do you expect Marius and Selene to be there?"

With a small tight exhale, he answers. "What I hope for and what I expect are two different things." He briefly looks around but does return his focus to me. "Marius is an exceptionally good tracker. If anyone can rescue her without alerting her captors, it is he."

"I pray you're right. Selene is my best friend and I couldn't forgive myself if anything happened to her."

"You mentioned that Lady V dislikes Selene. Other than Selene overhearing something she wasn't supposed to, there must be more to that story?"

I shrugged. "Grandmama dislikes any woman that she thinks attractive or beautiful. Selene's beautiful black hair, ivory skin, and classic features intimidate many."

He narrows his eyes. "That cannot be the real reason."

"I promise you Grandmama is quite territorial about being the most attractive woman. When I first met Selene, I was intimidated that a woman so beautiful would want to be friends with me." Looking ahead at the road I recognize for the first time that I pity Grandmama's insecurities. "I worried that Selene only wanted to be friends with me due to my status."

"Do you often feel that way?"

"I suppose."

Like he just discovered the answer to a riddle, he draws out the first word. "That's explains why you preferred to hide in the library."

Whirling to face him, I expected to find him smiling in a teasing manner, but his tone was matter of fact. I wished I knew what he meant. Did he mean that I am self-conscious? And hide from life? That I am unsuited for the role of princess and future queen? Wishing

I had the confidence to reply with a clever quip, I say nothing and look back towards Lena who is talking with Dominik.

"I'll rejoin Lena." I turned the horse and fled.

\#

We reach the base of the cliffs before nightfall. I've only ascended the cliffs from the south. With Gisela and Lena, I'll only attempt the climb with daylight. There is no sign of Marius, so we camp for the evening.

Gisela and I sit by the fire once everyone had gone to sleep. We haven't spoken privately about our unexpected encounter with the Owl. I've wanted to ask her what she learned from him. I haven't told the rest of the wolves that we met and spoke with the Owl. As he had said, the stories matter. And I'm loath to change the whispered lore. I also needed time to sort through my own feelings from what he told me about Gisela. Her abrupt departure this afternoon makes me think that I hurt her feelings.

Whether Gisela means for us to always have time by the fire alone, it doesn't matter. I look forward to it, now. I want to see her red hair glistened by the flames and moonlight. The shadows dance over the angles of her face. Her voice is direct yet sultry. There is no capriciousness in her nature. Unlike Lady V. Unless Gisela has surpassed her grandmother in the art of deceit. But my instincts tell me she is the direct opposite of a liar. Her comments about Selene were telling. Yes, Selene is a beautiful woman, but Gisela red hair, petite stature are equally if not more attractive. I also enjoy watching how every emotion she feels is expressed through her eyes and mouth.

"I apologize if I hurt your feelings earlier today."

She fidgets with her boot strings. "What did you mean by I 'hide in the library?'"

"That you don't want to create problems with Lady V. The library is most likely the safest place."

"I don't feel judged there."

"When did you want to learn the ancient languages?"

"When I was six. I wanted to study with my mother."

I stoked the fire with kindling. "How old were you when she died?

"Ten."

The orange, red, yellow, and black flames dance like ocean waves. I shiver and inch my hands closer towards the fire. In my tired gaze, my fingers and the flames nearly become one.

"I lost my mother when I was ten too." I added but afraid to look at her.

"I'm sorry."

"How did she die?"

"Childbirth . . . she and my sister didn't survive." Many years later my throat still clogs.

Tears shine in her eyes. "That is tragic to lose a mother and a sibling in the same day. I'm sor—"

"Don't say sorry. Life is unforgiving." I gaze at the sky and roll down the sleeves of my chamise. The temperature drops with each minute. I cross my arms over my chest and fixate on the dancing flames. The colors of orange, blue, and red blending seamlessly. "My father pleaded with God to save her. He made every promise he could. Nothing. God ignored every plea."

"Don't you think that God welcomed them into heaven."

"Yes," I croak, my tongue dry. "It never provided much comfort when I wanted to hug my mother and know my sister."

The blaze crackles. Owl had said I needed to put my life in God's hands. I've plotted for so long. Remained in control of myself and the wolves. How do I hand over control? It was asking near the impossible for me.

Above the stars danced without the veil of clouds. Was God looking down on us? Did He want to help me?

"I hoped I would find answers." Gisela breaks my reverie.

"What answers were you looking for?"

"What happened to my mother and how to help the kingdom. Grandmama encouraged it. Saying I would help her unite everyone."

I want my eyes to roll. Imagine saying that to a young girl who lost both her parents. That must be the protocol for Gisela. How could she be useful? Nothing else about her mattered. Not her sweetness, intelligence, spunk, natural beauty. I had imagined many ways that I would bring Lady V to justice for what she did to my family, but now there was one more person I wanted to avenge.

"Was reading and studying all that Lady V encouraged you to do?"

"Yes. But I failed her. I couldn't find the location of the red diamond and documents gave conflicting histories."

"How is that failing her? I'd say the issue is that the information doesn't exist."

The wind blows a little harder and the flames lean eastward as her hair blows towards me. The scent of lilacs reminds me of when I found her in the meadow.

"I've spent so much time in the library that I wasn't paying attention to life outside." She hesitated "Grandmama is not a well-regarded leader, is she?"

Before I have time to formulate an answer without completely giving my biased opinion, faint sounds tickle the small hairs on the back of my neck. I stand and make ready with my sword. I mime an archer stance to Gisela. She pulls an arrow from the quiver on her back and notches it into her bow. Pulling back the string ready to release the arrow depending upon who enters our camp. A reminiscent whistle comes from the same direction as the first sound. I answer and from the returning call, I close my eyes and take a deep inhalation of relief knowing who it is.

With a brief grateful glance upward thanking God, I then see Marius and Selene appear from behind a formation of rocks. Gisela runs to embrace Selene and I too hug my best friend. I surveyed them. Selene appears exhausted with bags under her eyes and slightly swaying on her feet. Marius vibrates with suppressed energy and simmering anger judging by his clenched fists. Dried mud cakes their clothes. What kind of adventure did they have?

I look to Gisela. "Why don't you help her to your tent, and we can talk in the morning?"

She nods and guides Selene away. Selene leans her head on Gisela's shoulder, which is rather comical given the height difference between them. But I'm also touched by their friendship.

While I am grateful and relieved that Marius rescued Selene and returned to us, I am also disappointed to be robbed of time with Gisela to discuss our conversations with the Owl. Is she as confused as I about her conversation with the Owl?

Marius' eyes follow Selene as she walks away to her tent. When the flap closes, he turns to me. That look of yearning on his face is comical. And I'd tease him if I weren't also starting to feel a twinge of it too. But for the other lady.

I slap his shoulder. "I can't wait to hear the story."

Marius laughs but runs his fingers through his hair and pours himself some tea that was kept warm by the fire.

"I'm not sure where to begin, but I'm positive someone is trailing us."

I smiled, Soon everything would come to head. "I hope it's Hugo."

"Do you want more on guard duty?"

"No, that will alert him. We proceed as planned but keep an eye out." I know to never let my guard down with Hugo and Lady V. Once was enough.

#

My pulse spikes as I observed the two figures by the fire. Once they returned to their tents, I silently snuck back to my camp about a quarter of a mile away.

Had Lady V allowed me to interview this Rolf before she hired him, then I could have saved my men and I this journey. Her instincts weren't off when she asked me to trail Gisela and Rolf. Or rather His Highness, Prince Max of Moritz. Max slipped through my fingertips all these years and now here he was. I had to fight every instinct in me to wait for him to be asleep and then finally eliminate the last of the Moritz line.

Sending only one man to retrieve the Lady Selene caught my huntsmen off guard but they were able to track him and Selene once he rescued her from the dwarves. Lady V would have to repair that relationship if she wanted the dwarves to continue supplying the kingdom with selenium. I was used to Lady V's jealous nature with other young attractive young women, but as far as I knew Selene had not done anything to capture the eye of a man that Lady V wanted. And how interesting that Max was enamored with Gisela. Wasn't that news! Yes, this could work to our advantage.

I reach camp and a huntsmen salutes. "The huntsmen are ready, Sir Hugo. Shall we attack after midnight?"

I shake my head and roll my eyes at this young huntsman. I needed to add patience to the training regime. "No, we will follow them and attack at the right moment...When I say so!"

He bows as he backs away. "Yes sir."

Begrudgingly I admit Max has been a worthy opponent. His father would be proud. My training as a wolf under Prince Ansgar was a privilege but Lady V's offer to defect was far too enticing to pass up. The huntsmen are now elite warriors due to the skill set I learned from wolf training. Switching allegiances was difficult but necessary. I owe my status to myself and any way to gain power I will do it. I lay down close to the fire dreaming about tomorrow. So many times, Max eluded me and this time I vowed he will not escape me. The only hindrance that concerns me is Gisela. What to do with her if she gets in the way?

Chapter 7

The cliffs of Acillion are shades of reddish clay with sharp spires that make it impossible for man to climb. Passed down through my family is the only known way to reach the only plateau where my family's main castle once stood. It was a perfect location. The cliffs have no beach below for any ship to land except for one hidden cove. Then from the lookout towers of the castle the guards could see for miles any scouts attempting to sneak through the Thuringian Forest. The forest was so dense that no army could penetrate. Except when a disgraced wolf pack warrior betrayed us. And set in motion the downfall of my family and dynasty.

With that depressing and infuriating thought pushing me onward, I looked back to see that everyone was keeping up on the steep climb. By this point the slope required everyone to walk beside their horses. Marius brings up the rear ensuring that no one or thing can sneak up on us. Then the other wolves, Dominik, Ludovic, and Kaspar in front of Marius. They focus on surveying the right and left directions in case of attack. Just in front of the wolves Gisela deftly holds three sets of reins. Leading her, Lena's, and Selene's horses while Lena holds

Selene up with an arm around her waist and Selene's arm over Lena's shoulders.

"Selene, I'm sure Marius would be happy to carry you," Lena says.

I turned, waiting for Selene's response.

Her cheeks flush. "I'm fine." She hobbled over to me. When did she hurt her ankle?

Her voice pleading and edged with pain and exhaustion. "Please don't bother Marius. I promise I will keep up."

I looked to Marius who observed us. His usual friendly expression is now inscrutable. We discussed all facts. The dwarves kidnapped Selene with aid from the Huntsmen. Why? We are still not sure.

I trust that Marius provided every detail about the rescue, but I know he's leaving out something. What happened to make Marius brood? I'm positive that Marius has feelings for Selene. But Selene is harder to read. Maybe tonight as we sit by the fire, I can ask Gisela if she knows.

"I'll put you onto my horse for the rest of the way. We only have two miles to go."

After I lift Selene onto Deimhein, I see Gisela out of the corner of my eye. The worry in her expression makes me concerned. Her grandmother sent her out into the world with little training, hired a guide out of the blue, expected her to place her life in the guide's (my) hands, find the Owl, (rather he found us), and then find the red diamond. While being told her whole life, she was useless. Now her best friend was kidnapped and from the look of it, still suffering from that experience. Lady V had to have something to do with it. Otherwise, why would the huntsmen be involved? Gisela may be a bit of a brat but she certainly had grit to silently stand up to Lady V all these years.

The rest of the journey to the plateau is quiet and uneventful. Once we reach the top everyone walks closer to the edge of the cliffs to admire the view. There is nothing but a magnificent blue horizon ahead. Below the sheer drop, the ocean meets the rocks. My grandfather had spoken about this view, but his poetic remembrance still doesn't prepare me for the majestic beauty before me. I peer over towards Gisela who for the first time since I've met her wears a smile of unabashed happiness. The wind whips her hair all around her head. I'm captivated watching something so innocent. The golden orange glow of the afternoon sun sets her hair ablaze and I am like a moth drawn to it.

My heart tells me she is not Lady V, but my mind is still apprehensive about the granddaughter of the woman that destroyed my family's kingdom.

Gisela peers over at me. "Do we have time to search for the Crimson palace?"

"You cannot wait until morning?" I tease. Though I too am eager to search.

"Nope." She smiles.

I instruct Ludovic and Kaspar to set up the camp while the rest of us explore up to a five-mile radius.

"We will pair off. If you find something whistle."

The others walk off in their pairs and Gisela stands there watching me.

"I assume you meant for me to pair with you." She smiled mischievously. "Or rather so you could keep an eye on me."

"The thought had crossed my mind. And while your reading skills must far outpace mine, I don't know about your whistling ability."

"I never knew you had a sense of humor."

I bow a flair and gesture for her to lead the way. "On occasion I too like to laugh."

The lighthearted banter is refreshing and softens me. Yet I won't let my guard down knowing that someone is following us and could decide to attack us at any minute. We search through the overgrown trees and bushes.

"I assume you were not expecting a real live man to be the Owl."

"No." She sighs as she moves branches away from her face as we walk further into the forest. The greenery is so dense that a stag could have been five yards away and we would never know. "I wish I had more time with him. I could live in that library."

I pull up a large limb so she can duck underneath. Putting my hand on her shoulder I'm struck by her striking scarlet cloak and her auburn hair. Most of the journey she tied it in a bun at the base of her neck but today it is down in loose waves around her shoulders. Like the night we danced together. As my eyes travel from my hand on the cloak up her neck to her face, I see that she is watching me. Neither of us moves except for breathing. Underneath my hand her body trembles. Do I frighten her? The whites of her eyes widen, and her mouth is slightly open to release her many shaky breaths.

"You're trembling. Why?"

She shook her head, but we didn't break eye contact and remained standing so close together. As I imagine myself pulling her into my arms, I strive to break the trance and step back.

I cleared my throat, "Did he answer any of your question about your mother?" I walk ahead afraid of standing too close to her now. I look back when she doesn't answer immediately. "Are you coming?"

Gisela hadn't moved. She blinked and rushed forward. "Yes, sorry." Her gait a little faster and with intention. "I didn't get a chance to ask many questions. I let the Owl talk."

"So did I." While I want to share something about my chat, I know I cannot share everything the Owl told me. I am just Rolf to her. Not Prince Max of Moritz.

"He said that God sent me a warrior." She tells me this softly as she looks in all directions but at me,.

I want to tell her that she is safe to share this with me. That I won't use it against her. Yet I *am* lying to her.

She catches my arm to turn me towards her. "And that I'll have to trust him even when my heart doesn't want to."

Thank you, Lord. Please increase my guilt. I turn my face away from her to scowl at the irony. I've been trying my whole life to repair the havoc her family reaped on mine and yet I am quickly becoming the guilty party for hiding my identity from Gisela.

"Rolf."

I turned my head back to face her. Hoping that any traces of anger had left my face.

"I do trust you." She leaned up on tiptoe which only reached my jawline and gave me a kiss. I am completely disarmed.

"Gisela—"

A piercing whistle interrupts me, coming from the west of us.

"They must have found something! Hurry!"

Off she goes before I can stop her dashing around trees and under branches. I rush after her somewhat grateful for the interruption but knowing that eventually I'll have to say something. Whether it is telling her the truth about my identity I'm not sure. All I know is that I cannot give up my quest no matter how my feelings for her have changed.

\#

We found the Crimson Palace! Decades of abandonment have weakened the structure. Cobwebs spread out from the ceilings down the walls and over furniture. Walking through each room there are fallen beams and uneven flooring from the ivy, and growing trees expanding into every crevice. I try to picture what it could have looked like. The grand ballroom with banners hung from the rafters and musicians playing from the balcony above. Guards proudly watching from the turrets yet appreciating the views. Scrumptious food from the kitchens and the smell of fresh rosemary bread always brings the children to the kitchen in search of a slice. A library like the Owl's. Multiple levels of books, and a cozy fireplace with a chess board. I also imagine stained glass windows because the warmth of sunlight shining through colored glass can be so comforting. Grandmama did not want a library but allowed the space close to the dungeon to be used for research. It is cold, damp and has no windows at all.

Rolf and the other men explore the main hall. One of them tells the others to look for any extra swords or other weapons. Lena, Selene, and I decided to venture upstairs. The first step of the staircase crumbles as I step down on it, but I luckily don't fall through. I scan to see if the men heard anything, but they are focused on searching through other parts of the castle.

"Should we wait for them?" I asked warily, not wanting to annoy Rolf.

"I'm sure they'll be following us shortly." Selene assures.

Once we climbed the stairs, we came to a small room covered in dust. Lying open on the floor is a large leather-bound book. Before picking it up I crouch down and gently blow off some dust wanting to make sure no small insect has made a home in the book. Faint handwriting is legible now. I picked it up and began to read from the page that lay open.

3rd of April – I am heartbroken. How I wish my father had never brought her here. A new stepmother? When my dear mama has been gone barely a month. I will have to hide the red diamond somewhere where she cannot find it. Mama left instructions for me before she died. How could she have known that papa wasn't to be trusted?

6th of May – Strix finally arrived and helped me to ensure that Mama's wishes were carried out. I have only six more months until my birthday and his regency ends. He is frantic about producing a child with my stepmother. Strix advised me to outwit my father and to pray. I never dreamt that I would have to play the ultimate game of cat and mouse with my own father. I'll pray that God gives me the strength to not fall back on sentimentality. My mother is gone and as her heir the kingdom must be my priority.

I can't stop myself from reading. What if this was the diary of the Dragon Queen's great-granddaughter? I believed the story I read about the creation of the red diamond, but to many the fantastic conclusion was a bit harder to accept. The red diamond disappeared sometime during the reign of Queen Amelie. She came to the throne five years after her mother died, because her father tried to keep the throne as regent. A civil war ensued but eventually the rightful Queen prevailed.

I look up and inspect the room to see if any other books exist. The other shelves are empty. And nothing else on the floor. At the open window, a red and grey finch lands chirping, but I return to reading.

21st of October- I've just made the hardest decision of my life so far. I signed my papa's death warrant. My council wanted me to sign the death warrants for my stepmother and my half-brother, but I refuse to condemn them. Strix agrees that it is the right to spare them, but I cannot deny how torn I feel about this decision. Why did God choose me for this role? And why did he give me a father who sought to usurp the crown from me?

While I drank in every word, the finch flies once over me and then leaves. Soon the caw of a raven interrupts me while I'm reading. It flies down to the dusty floor and just watches me. Its black eyes appear lifeless. "Shoo!" It remains there, still, and ominous. I finally got up and chased it away as it's very presence watching me read was unnerving. I flip forward a few more pages.

12th of February- My pity and forgiveness were misplaced. My half-brother has raised an army. Bitterness and greed prevailed. Dear Lord, don't let it enter my heart. I want to spend this time with my husband and our newborn son. My dear Conrad has created an elite group of warriors called the wolves. They are meant to protect the kingdom of Moritz forever.

So, this was when the wolves originated. Hugo hated the wolves. I suppose because the wolves were the natural enemies of the huntsmen. But here it shows that it was the wolves that protected the sovereign and the kingdom. Why did that change?

All my life Grandmama, my tutors, and the Huntsmen shared how the people celebrated the end of the Moritz reign. But I had yet to find what made their reign so terrible. Could it be one more of her lies? My foundation is continually rocked and I'm ready for it to end. I want to know the truth. About everything.

20th of November- My half-brother is dead, but his daughter is proving to be a worse thorn in my side than her father or grandfather. I'm only sorry that I am near death and did not finish the job. I thought I was doing God's will and now my ancestors will have to pay for my mercy. At least the red diamond is safe forever and I know where Strix and I hid it will be safe until the right person comes along.

Who is Strix, I wonder. More importantly, I wish there were more clues about the red diamond.

24th of November- Strix came to see me today to formally say goodbye. I will miss my dear Owl. Just as I will miss Conrad, and Kenric. My son will have many challenges ahead but hopefully Conrad, the wolves, and Strix will guide him.

So, the Owl's name is Strix. As I wonder about Kenric and his reign, I hear the raven chortling outside. Strange, usually ravens prefer to be in a pair or pack. This one was solitary. The overwhelming urge to read to the last page controls me even though I have no idea how much time has lapsed and if Rolf is wondering where I am.

26th of November- This will be my last entry. The House of Moritz will survive without me. The red diamond will be kept safe in a place where the sun shines on the word.

'Where the sun shines on the word.' What could that mean? Could it be the Bible? A painting? Where would someone hide a diamond? How do I know that it was still here? No matter how implausible it seems to still be in this crumbling castle but if it had been found word would have spread throughout the kingdom faster than the strike of a lightning bolt.

Holding the diary in my hands I study the cover and just happen to turn it over and glance at the back. An intricately drawn sun covers the back. The rays spread out from the center to all four corners. The back cover is also thicker than the front. With careful study I notice that one corner of the fabric covering it curls back.

The thought of ripping a book horrifies me. But I can't stop myself. Inch by inch the fabric pulls away, reveling only black fabric. Then something shiny catches my eye. It is red like a ruby, but the sparkle is unparalleled. Could it be? Something thought lost for decades was hidden away in a diary. It is the size of an acorn. I always assumed it would be larger, but size never dictated the uniqueness of an item. I want to tell Lena and Selene first and then Rolf. I wrap the diamond up in a handkerchief and hide it in my vest pocket. As I call out for Lena and Selene, a battle horn rings out. Who could be attacking us?

Lena and Selene ran from the other room towards me. "Hurry we have to find Rolf and the others!"

We descend the stairs faster than we ascended. The men are running from room to room taking positions at windows or doorways. Rolf and Marius stomp towards us fuming. "Where have you been?"

"We are under attack!" They both shouted at us at the same time. Rolf grabs my hand dragging me away to hide behind an inner wall with only one window.

Breathless I ask, "Who is attacking us?"

His face still a mask of fury. "Your grandmother's huntsmen." And leaves before I can say anything else.

Chapter 8

Arrows flew through open windows, but I only hear the whoosh through the air. Crouched down I try to peek around the side of the wall, looking for Rolf.

Why is Hugo attacking us? If Grandmama did order them and the dwarves to kidnap Selene, then are they trying to kill her now?

I must make them stop.

"Selene. Lena. Follow me." We climbed out the back window. I hope that Selene and Lena will be safe there while I distract the others. "Stay here and don't move unless Rolf or one his men come and retrieve you." I run as fast as I can to take cover by some boulders.

Waiting for a few heartbeats, I dared to peep around my cover to see if I could identify any of the huntsmen that Rolf claimed the attackers to be. Rolf was right. As usual. I didn't know the name of every man, but I recognized the faces of the men that popped up to release arrows just as Rolf's men ducked once they fired their own arrows.

A yank on my cloak pulls me down as I hear cross words in my ear, "Are *you* determined to kill yourself?" *Rolf. Oh no.* Even though he whispered the words, I knew I was in trouble.

"I'm sorry, but I had to make sure it was the huntsmen." My explanation didn't alter his furrowed brow and flared nostrils. "If the huntsmen were responsible for kidnapping Selene, I wanted to lead them away from her."

"What if they kidnapped you instead?" He asked through clenched teeth.

"I am Lady V's granddaughter. Why would they kidnap me?" My hands punctuate every word.

"Because Lady V is not to be trusted."

I rolled my eyes.

"She ordered them to kidnap your best friend. What makes you think you're immune from her machinations?"

I stared at him. Annoyed yet in agreement with his assessment of Grandmama. "She hired you. Should I not trust you?"

His silence makes me wonder if I hit a nerve with my last question. Arrows continue to fly from many directions while his head swivels from the right and left. "Just remember your dear Grandmama sent you out here with no training to find the Owl and red diamond. I don't think she'd hesitate to use you for her own means. Now stay down." He grabs my hand and pulls me behind him through the bushes to his horse.

"What about Selene and Lena?"

"Marius and the others will take care of them." He climbs into the saddle and yanks me up behind him. Urging his horse to race away with a kick of his heels. Feeling like I'm about to fall off, my arms clasp around Rolf's middle bringing my right cheek to rest upon the spot between his shoulder blades.

"Where are we going?"

An arrow swished past us. Rolf spurred his horse faster and making a sharp left turn around an evergreen. "I was hoping to find someplace to hide you away, but they are more determined than usual to capture their prize."

"Then they're not here for Selene again?"

"Why don't you ask them?"

I turned my head to see ten riders and horses, all racing as frantically as us. "You need Marius and the others."

"You don't trust me?"

"Not when it's ten against two!" I try to hide the worry in seeping into my veins.

"I'll try not be offended by your lack of confidence." He commented dryly.

"Please, Rolf. I don't want anything to happen to you." His lips compress and eyebrows raised surprised that I would show concern for him.

The clouds overhead grow darker as a storm approaches. And the further we ride into the forest the denser the trees come together and the fog swirls around forcing me to squint to make out shapes. Thunder clashes above us. The horse rears and I lose my grip, falling to the ground. I've never enjoyed surprises and falling off Rolf's horse is startling to all my senses. Landing in a holly bush with sharp branches and pointed leaves makes me feel like I've fallen into a bed of nails.

Before my head stops spinning, Rolf circles back and jumps down to help me out of the holly bush. Another thunderclap splits the air. His horse runs deeper into the forest.

As I stand there getting my bearing, Rolf pulls leaves and twigs from my hair. His hands then clasp my cheeks. "Are you alright?"

Droplets of rain touched down on our heads as the rumble of hooves alerted us to the arrival of our pursuers.

Hugo sat proudly atop his horse, back straight as a board on his horse. His grin so wide that I wondered if his lips will split open.

"What a merry chase you've led us on, Gisela."

As the granddaughter of the ruler a modicum of respect was bestowed upon me. While I was given the opportunity to always question if they respected me or just wanted to use me. I never used those times to assert my own dominance. Now, in this time I needed to at least question what someone I had always given respect, was doing to harm me and my friends. If there was ever a time in my life to show strength and dominance it was now. "Hugo, what do you mean by attacking Rolf, his men, Selene, Lena, and me?"

He shifted his attention towards Rolf, pulling his sword from his scabbard, leveling it at us, my heart leapt into my throat. His menacing gaze startling me.

"You're under arrest for lying to Lady V."

"What are you talking about?" I look back and forth between Hugo and Rolf.

Though Rolf did not look surprised at Hugo's statement.

"I do admire your plan. It was ingenious to involve Gisela."

Rolf protested with a shout. "She knows nothing."

I'm flabbergasted as to what Hugo meant. But I forced myself to remain calm, wanting to draw out his accusation against me.

He clucked his tongue, as his eyes shifted back to me for a moment but returned to Rolf. "Hiding information like your Grandmama. How sad she will be when she finds out that her heir is plotting to overthrow her."

My brow furled stunned by his words. "What are you talking about?"

Hugo spoke to me but his wording was strange, like he was speaking to his comrades. "The Lady Gisela and Prince Max working together. Who would have thought it?"

I turned my gaze to Rolf to seek reassurance that my conclusion that Hugo had lost his mind is correct. But Rolf's glare at Hugo is so full of retribution that a sinking feeling in my stomach made me worried.

"I've never met Prince Max. And even if I had I wouldn't work with him to overthrow Grandmama." I wanted to smack the smug expression from Hugo's face.

"That's where you're wrong." Hugo spits out. His smug smile directed at Rolf. "Your plan was brilliant, Max. It was clever to use Gisela. Especially when Lady V announced at her party that she would send out Gisela to find the Owl. It was the perfect opportunity to bring back the House of Moritz. But the Huntsmen have finally found the wolf."

Rolf is Prince Max? *Please dear God. No*. His father killed my mother. All those nights around the fire when I shared my hopes and feelings about my past. He. Lied. To. Me.

I tug on his arm to face me. I want my voice to remain stoic and clear, but I'm sure my emotions are easily escaping and showing themselves with a hoarse voice. "Please. Tell me he is lying."

"He isn't." His shoulders slumped. "I am Prince Maximilian Rudolf Wilhem Moritz of Cadmium."

Hugo snorted. "And you'll both answer for your crimes."

Max pulled his sword and stepped in front of me. "You'll have to go through me first." There is an edge to Max's voice that I've never heard before. And the next word sounded as if he were spitting out a bug that somehow found its way into his mouth. "Traitor!"

I stepped away from Max needing to put some distance between us. He was supposed to be different. Someone who didn't use me. Was he acting the whole time?

While Hugo and Rolf volleyed insults back and forth, I studied the other huntsmen who all had their bows notched with arrows. Ready to release them at any moment. For the first time I worried about how we would escape. Unless Rolf—Max's men were on their way to save us. Every second seemed interminable. I needed an explanation from Max, but that would have to wait.

"You will come with us now!" Hugo ordered.

Max raised his sword. "I. Think. Not."

The twitch of a bow from one of the archers caught my attention and without thinking I made myself a shield for Max just as the impact of an arrow through my shoulder pinned me into him. He held me as my legs buckled to the ground. But the pain and shock turned my vision to black as I heard Max yell out "NO!"

#

I caught Gisela as she fell back against me. The impact of the arrow sluicing through her skin and muscle. It's so intense that the tip just pierced my doublet. Falling to my knees, I eased her down as gently as possible. I cradled her in my arms and called out her name. No response comes and turning her head to see that she has passed out, makes me yell out, "No! Gisela. Wake up!" *As if that will do anything.* I've completely lost any sense. This little redheaded imp has become my reason.

The blood streaming out both ends of the wound scares me so much that I've conveniently forgotten about Hugo and the other huntsmen, letting down my guard. Any one of them could have finished me off with one thrust of their sword. Hugo stands above us, his mouth open, and a stricken look on his face, despite his earlier threats.

"Don't just stand there! We need to get the arrow out and dress her wound."

None of the huntsmen make any move. Until Hugo then grabs a rolled-up bandage from his saddle bag. I scrutinized Gisela's limp body to ensure she had no other wounds and that her breathing wasn't erratic. I'm awed by what she's come to mean to me, in this brief time. After I had lied to her, she still saved me.

I got to work on extracting the arrow and stalled the flow of oozing blood from the wound. All while the huntsmen stood over watching. Mixtures of disinterest and impatience on their faces. Without Gisela, I would have fought my way out, but I wasn't going to leave her. If—when she woke up, I had to explain myself. I owed her that at least.

"Time to go, Your Highness." A huntsmen pushes the tip of his sword into the middle of my back. I collected Gisela and carried her towards Hugo.

A raven circles above us and lands once Hugo lifts his forearm. He slips a note into the tube secured to its leg, strokes its back, and pushes it off to fly. That must be how he and Lady V were communicating. I'll admit I am put out that Hugo attacked sooner than I expected and I find myself and Gisela their prisoners, but the wolves and I had not survived all these years by not using impossible situations to our advantage. I just needed to find when I could press the advantage with Gisela.

The sword at my back nudges me to follow Hugo as he and his horse proceed down another path from the cliffs. I'd never known about this path.

"Am I expected to carry Gisela the whole journey back?"

"Not at all." Hugo didn't turn. "We have something to bring you back to the Scarlet Palace. All in good time, Max."

If I can keep him bellowing like that, maybe Marius and the other wolves will hear.

"Is that how you tracked us? The Raven."

"Yes. She knew something was odd about you."

"It must make you furious knowing I and all the wolves were able to sneak in and out of that ball with no one suspecting anything."

As much as it was to annoy him, I needed to keep him talking if that would help the wolves locate us. I also needed help from Selene or Lena in taking care of Gisela. Her cheeks are no longer healthy pink but pale and clammy. Her body was hot to the touch as her body fought the infection.

"I've waited long enough to capture you and the wolves. And this time all of you will pay."

"What did my family ever do to have you betray them like you did? My father trained you himself."

"I was never going to be the leader of the wolves. That role was only for you, the heir. I was continually passed over for other roles and Lady V is quite generous to her loyal subjects."

"What did the Wolves ever do to you?"

"They follow your lead. It is simpler to eradicate them."

"What makes you think you'll catch them?"

"I left a few surprises."

Who knew what kind of trouble that could be? In other words, I was on my own, for a little while, until everyone could catch up to us. But again, when was anyone's guess. For now, I'd have to wait, plot, watch over Gisela, and take advantage of an escape when I could and Gisela's safe.

By the next hour, my arms were fighting fatigue from carrying Gisela. We were a hundred yards from the bottom of the cliffs when I saw their 'wagon.' A crude prison wagon. Bars on all sides. Not at all comfortable but at least I could make up a bed for Gisela to rest in where she could recover.

Once we entered our traveling prison the huntsmen rarely speak to me. My days are filled with ensuring that Gisela is comfortable. A challenging task with no medicine and the rickety bumps that disturb her when the wagon wheels travel over rocks or in ditches. She alternated between sweating and shivering through most days and nights. Her red hooded cloak came in handy to keep her warm. The wooden floor of our prison provided no comfort.

By the third night, Gisela's pulse grew faint and her breathing erratic. Lying down next to her, I caressed her face, internally pleading with her to open her eyes. Moisture gathered in my eyes, and I decided to talk to her even though I wasn't sure if she'd remember anything.

"I'm sorry for hiding my identity. But I had no choice. The plan was to use you and then take back my throne. What I didn't plan on was you. You with your ability to see the positive in any situation, your spunk, zest for life, intelligence, and loyalty." Fingering her beautiful auburn hair, I loved watching it in the sunlight or by the fire. She captivated me for her mind and beauty.

A harsh shudder released my lungs. "Watching every sunset and every sunrise with you for the rest of my life will never be enough," I whispered into her ear.

Not even her eyelids flickered. I pulled her closer into my arms. I closed my eyes and silently prayed. Something I hadn't done since my mother's death. Would God hear me? The Owl made me wish so. I was prepared to make any deal I could with God. He just couldn't take away Gisela.

I awoke and it was still night outside. Gisela is still in arms, and I still feel the fever burning through her.

"Psst."

I searched for the source. No one was there.

"Psst. Max."

I glanced at the roof of the wagon, and it was a blackbird. I sat up as he flew down to land on my knee.

"The Owl sent me. He wanted me to remind you that God is with you."

"Please tell the Owl, thank you. But I desperately need medicine for Gisela. She's dying."

He raises one wing, and underneath is a small vial with a mixture of green herbs. "He sent this. It should relieve the fever and infection. Make a small compress and have her drink the rest. But give it to her quickly. She does not have much time."

As he was about to fly off, he turned back to me. "Take heart, Your Highness. We all want Lady Gisela to live. It is you who must find faith and not give up hope. That is the only way she will survive. Only together..." He flew off through the bars to the pitch-black night.

Her survival depended upon me. God was truly testing me now. I prepared the compress and mixed a portion of the herbs with the water. Tipping her head back to make her drink. I remove her vest, and a rock fell out of the pocket. Picking it up I'm struck my its color and brilliance. The deep red and unpolished appearance made me think it was a rock but now studying it I see it is not a rock but a diamond. The red diamond that Gisela had hidden in her vest and never told me. I squeezed my fist around it like my heart had a band tightening around it to the point of suffocation. What hursts beyond measure is wondering if she ever planned to tell me.

Chapter 9

I sat on the ice-cold stone floor of my dungeon cell fuming and worried. A disconcerting combination. The bottom cell deep in the depths of the castle, my spirits reciprocated its elevation. No sunlight to welcome dawn. Alone with my memories and thoughts. Marius and the wolves would come for me, of that I was certain. But it was thoughts of Gisela, our future, and the crown that consumed me.

Even though the blackbird told me to have faith and hope in Gisela, it was the most difficult challenge of my life. Yes, I wanted her to have faith in me. I struggled with trusting others. I had so many reasons to be angry with God. He took my parents, little sister, and grandfather. He allowed Lady V to take the crown. Every year I lived to restore what was stolen from me.

The red diamond was the key to longevity and a peaceful reign. In a moment of weakness, I squirreled it into a secret compartment in my boot. I now regretted the hasty action. The all-consuming emotions of securing my throne took over me.

I had already lied to Gisela about my identity, and now I never gave her the chance to tell her she'd found the red diamond. I wanted to punch the stone walls of the dungeon. The Owl was right. I wasn't allowing God to guide me. I was trying to control my own destiny. But it was all I knew. When would I learn to trust?

I got up and paced. To walk the entire cell only required thirty steps. Walking the cell was the only physical activity I had at that moment. It would have to do.

The cell door slammed backward. Two jailers stood at the entrance. They stepped aside and bowed as the lady who caused my nightmares walked through.

"Max. Dear little Max. Look how you've grown into a handsome man." She eyed me up and down like I was piece of horseflesh to place a wager on for a race. Her pressed lips into a tight smile like a cat cornering a mouse. Let her think she won for now.

"Thank you, Lady V." I bow at the waist wanting to return her form of sarcasm. "Where is your self-important dunderhead?"

Her eyebrows flatten and her lips pursed. Hopefully in annoyance.

"After all, you've never accomplished anything without the men you've managed to manipulate all these years."

"Like your father and grandfather." She walks closer and while I was able to pick the lock on my manacles just before she arrived, I kept my hands behind my back . She cupped my cheek and racked her nails down to my jawbone.

"You've been busy."

I jerked my face out of her talons. "Not busy enough."

"Oh, come now, you managed to evade my huntsmen for ten years, you tricked me into believing you were Rolf, the simple guide." She glanced around the room. "And most important of all my granddaughter fell in love with you."

I was glad that Lady V didn't have the power to see my elated heart pounding faster. I allowed one eyebrow to lift to show mild interest. I did not want her to know my actual feelings for Gisela. "It was quite simple to charm a naïve young woman into loving a wolf." My smile is brittle and hurts my face. "But you wanted to keep Gisela ignorant of the truth. She would be much easier to manipulate that way."

Lady V's irises widened a tiny bit.

"If you planned to use her to reclaim the throne, it won't work."

My teeth clenched. "I never planned on using her."

"How else would you have found the red diamond?"

"Who said we did?"

"If someone had not found the red diamond, the raven would not have summoned the Huntsmen to attack."

"Your huntsmen that were supposed to protect Gisela?" I asked trying to understand her level of maliciousness.

"Who said they were to protect her?" Her laugh echoed throughout the chamber.

It kept her distracted and vulnerable to surprises. "I have one question."

"What is it?"

"Were the huntsmen and dwarves meant to kidnap Selene or Gisela?"

"Selene." Her smile minimized . Folding her hands in front of her, she watched me. "Aren't you going to ask me why?"

My lips formed a crooked smile. "You fear beautiful or intelligent woman and eliminate anyone that threatens your ego."

Her nostrils flared. "I have two options. Allow Hugo to torture you or just hang you."

"I'd prefer to hang."

She huffed and stomped out of the room, her long fabric train trailing behind her. The sound of the fabric on the floor reminded me of a weaving through grass.

I rubbed my hands over my face and hair. I needed to find Gisela, but I had to wait for the wolves.

My head turned when I overheard some scuffles and groans. A guard walked through the doorway followed by Marius holding a sword to his back. He ordered the guard to unlock the cell door.

"What took you so long?"

He smirked. "I hope you've enjoyed your stay at the Scarlet Palace, but I think you need a new room."

Once I'm through the cell, Marius knocked the guard unconscious with the heel of his sword. The rest of the wolves drag in the other unconscious guards, tie them up, and secure them all in one cell.

Overjoyed to see my pack all alive and unharmed, I hugged each of them. Selene and Lena stood at the back, their eyes wide and fingers clenched together.

"What news of Gisela?" I asked.

"We know nothing." Marius answered. "I was afraid to let them sneak upstairs and blow our cover."

Selene glared at Marius.

"We will check on her soon." I pat her shoulder.

"What is your plan?" Ludovic asked.

"I'll go upstairs and take care of Lady V. Marius, Selene, and Lena find Gisela. The rest of you take out the guards and huntsmen." I pulled out the red diamond from the compartment in my boot. "Send word that Prince Max has returned with the red diamond."

\#

The harsh sunlight stung my eyes as I awoke. I tried to pull up the quilted covers but moving my arm proved impossible. Cracking my eyelids open a white bandage wrapped my right shoulder. What happened? How did I get here?

As my eyes adjusted to the light, I realized I was in my room back at Scarlet Palace. Everything in my room was exactly as it was when I'd left. Or did I dream about everything? My bookcases, my desk, and my red cloak now hung over the armoire. The last thing I remembered was facing Hugo and the other huntsman with Rolf— no Rolf never existed. Rolf was Prince Max. My breath caught thinking of him. Those evenings by the fire. When I opened my heart and mind to him. Had he been truthful to me? My chapped lips told me that I should save any hydration my body retained. Yet tears still formed at the corners of my eyes ready to fall.

Where was he? Please Lord, let him be well. If I was here, I hoped he hadn't been taken prisoner—or worse. No. Grandmama would want to make an example of him.

A tension headache brewed in my temples. I had to find him.

Contemplating getting up from bed was a herculean effort. I didn't know how many days I'd been asleep. My limbs ached. I shook my head further, clearing the cobwebs from my mind. My throat pleaded for water and my stomach grumbled.

As if my grumbling stomach was a bell to ring for a maid, the door opened and in came a household maid carrying a breakfast tray.

"Good afternoon, my lady." After she fluffed the pillows to help me sit up, she sat down with the tray preparing to spoon-feed me some broth with flower petals.

"Please that won't be necessary. I can use my other arm."

She nodded, keeping her eyes downward, not providing any chance for me to read her reaction. Neither Grandmama nor Hugo had come to visit yet, so she was my first chance to ask for information.

"How long was I asleep?"

"Three days, my lady."

"Are Lady V or Sir Hugo at the castle?"

"Yes."

"Was anyone else brought?" I had to pretend like I didn't care. I didn't know this maid and where her allegiances lay.

She eyed the food tray, and I grabbed the piece of toast.

"He captured Prince Max. And put him in the dungeon."

Just chew the toast. Don't react. "And have Lady Selene and Lady Lena returned?"

"No."

"Thank you. I'm finished."

"Are you sure? Lady V wanted to inspect the tray after you had eaten."

Well, that ruined my appetite knowing Grandmama issued orders for me to eat. "Alright I will try to eat a bit more. You don't watch me. I'll ring the bell when I'm done."

She bit her lip, but didn't protest and left the room. I had no idea what was going on and what Hugo shared with Grandmama. I couldn't sit here and try to eat when worry ate away at my nerves. When I tried to stand up from the bed my head swirled, and I flopped back down on the bed. I needed to find out where Max was and talk to him, but in my weak state standing up was proving to be difficult. Then I remembered the red diamond.

I sat up in a rush and held my head hoping the room would stop spinning. Frantic to find the diamond I made my way to my clothes and checked my vest. Nothing. Where was it? Had Max found it? I would prefer that. Rather than one of the maids finding it and giving it to Grandmama. I had to speak to Max.

Breakfast forgotten; I grab my red cloak, the only piece of clothing that would cover my nightgown. One bookcase hid a secret stairwell that travelled all the way down to the first level of the dungeon. It was the only way to get there undetected by the huntsmen. My heartbeat raced with the exertion to shuffle-walk in my weakened state. I couldn't wait. There was too much at stake. I only took a few steps before I fainted, falling to the floor.

\#

Hugo sat across from me drinking Madeira, while I sipped tea in my crimson sitting room. He beamed. I only saw a pathetic puppy looking for reassurance and praise for his loyalty. I resisted the urge to roll my eyes. It had taken him over ten years to capture Max. That was no reason to gloat. Frankly, if Max pledged loyalty to me, I would make him the leader of the huntsmen and dispose of Hugo.

How I wanted to sing! For the first time in many years the crown would finally be mine. Prince Max was locked up. Gisela lay near death.

"Have you checked on Gisela?"

"No, my lady. The maid took her breakfast."

"Very good. It shouldn't be long then until we hear from the maid." I checked the clock. "Where did the maid put the wildflowers?"

"In her oatmeal."

"You fool! She'll see the wildflowers there!"

"Relax, my lady. She hasn't eaten in over six days. She'll be ravenous."

I want to smack him. Rather I clench my fists. My sharp fingernails about to draw blood in my palms. *You only must suffer him a little longer*. But clearly, I should have supervised this myself.

My sitting room filled with cushions and charms kept me calm. But Hugo presence sorely taxed that calm.

"If she survives, I will hold you responsible." I took a deep breath. It had taken most of my life, but all my plans were finally coming to fruition. Except for one crucial piece. Gisela. One more a family member betrayed me. Gisela was too much like her mother. Too much integrity. Her mother had turned my son against me. That was the ultimate unforgivable sin.

"What do you plan to do with Max?" Hugo eyes.

The previous night Hugo and I discussed Max and Gisela.

"They rode like the devil was on their heels. Max almost eluded us but then Gisela fell off the horse from a sharp turn." Hugo paused. "Max turned back for her."

"Really?" One of my fingers tapped my cheek while I explored the possibility of a connection between Max and Gisela.

"After we cornered them, she threw herself in front of him to take the arrow."

None of the huntsmen had impressive skills. "Are you sure they didn't aim at her?"

"The archer claims if she hadn't been there, the arrow would have gone through his heart."

I wave my hand in a shooing motion. The protest of the archer who shot my granddaughter is immaterial. "I'll need to press her for information about Max."

"Good luck." He snorts. "I think Gisela is lost to you forever."

An eyebrow lifted at his odd comment. "Why would you say that?"

"No woman shields a man she's not in love with."

My blood ran cold. Was she in love with Max? He was handsome, yes, but Gisela should have known better. Men were meant to be used. I kept men from Gisela for that reason.

As a new strategy formulated in my mind, the satisfaction pinged throughout my body. "Do you know if they found the Owl or the red diamond?"

"The raven summoned us which was why we attacked. But when Gisela got sick, we had no opportunity to search her or Max. Once we arrived the huntsmen searched Max but found nothing on him or Gisela."

I crossed my arms. "I'm sure your search was extensive. The raven would not have summoned you for nothing."

He clears his throat. "Speaking as the leader of the huntsmen, I think you must solve the Gisela problem."

"What would you suggest?" Not that I'll take his advice, but listening to his words wouldn't cost me anything.

Hugo's hand slapped the table three times. The Madeira gave him false courage.

Scrunching my lips, I refocus. "I will go down to the dungeon and have a talk with Max before I decide my next move."

Frantic knocks at the door turned my attention to the maid that shuffles in. Her head bent low when she curtsied and remained facing down when she stood.

"Forgive me my lady, I brought Lady Gisela her breakfast tray, but when I left, she had only eaten the toast. I peeked around the door just now and she had put on her red cloak."

Hugo muttered an expletive, stood up and clumsily pulled out his sword.

"Put that away!" I took another sip of . "I have an idea where she was going."

Hugo looked at me with a blank expression.

"The dungeon." I supplied. "Bring her to me."

They scurried out, and I rolled my eyes. I supposed the poisoning would have to wait, for now.

I lifted my cup. Cold steel met my neck. I dropped the teacup and gasped.

"Don't move Lady V. Your day of reckoning has come."

#

When I woke, my head throbbed from falling on the stone floor. I massaged the ball of inflamed skin. Hugo swayed over me. I couldn't decipher his muttering as he leaned down to pull me up to stand next to him. His hand tightened around my bicep and dragged me through my room. No matter how I stumbled, nothing ceased his progress. "Where are you taking me?"

"To Lady V's. You have some explaining to do."

I was too weak to escape his grip. Loathing filled my stomach. Now, I could also add weak of spirit to my list of faults. I wanted to be strong in both mind and body. Like Max. Now, I had to face Grandmama alone. That thought filled me with dread, because there was no conceivable way for me to deny that I loved Max.

Chapter 10

It would be so simple to slit her throat. I was very tempted. Yet, in one moment of madness I could ruin years of plotting. Killing Lady V now would be immensely satisfying. Not only for the wrongs done to my family, my people, and me, but to Gisela. No one deserved a family member that made them feel insignificant and worthless. Knowing what she endured upset me more than my own past.

While my temper escalated, I thought then of the Owl and his advice that I needed to be a warrior for God. Let the Lord's guidance drive my actions. I finally understood what he meant. My anger and thirst for revenge against Lady V drove every decision. What would I do when this chapter was over? What would I do without the anger? It had become a sickness I couldn't shake. And what kind of king would I be if I let anger drive every decision?

"Stand up."

She followed my instructions, and I guided her over to a mirror. "Look at yourself one last time. Where I'll put you, there'll be no mirrors to feed your vanity."

She gulped and her eyes widened while her lips trembled.

Hopefully in fear, I will see this order carried out to the letter.

"Please just kill me now." She pleaded.

A harsh laugh escaped. "No. I will make this as long and painful for you as it was for me." I found a stripe of fabric and gagged her mouth. Then located the rope in my satchel and then bound her hands and feet.

Someone pounded their fist three times in quick succession on the door, "Lady V!"

Lady V tried to yell through the fabric gag. I pressed the tip of the knife closer to her jugular. Droplets of blood pooled where the tip pierced her skin, and she ceased her muffled cries.

In my best falsetto voice, I called out. "Who is it?"

"Hugo. I have Gisela."

"Mmmmfffmmm!" Lady V tried again to raise the alarm that something was amiss.

Using the knob on the end of the dagger I bob her on the top of her head to knock her unconscious.

"Wait!" I continued in the falsetto. "I am unwell."

I found a wooden hope chest and locked her in. My pulse raced as Hugo's knocking continued. I was ready to knock Hugo a few times for his poor listening skills. Looking around the room, I needed something to cover my face or shroud it. A five o'clock shadow was distinctly masculine and very noticeable. I tore through the closet for a veil or shawl. I selected a woolen shawl and doused all the candles except one far in the other corner. Then I drew the bed curtains and jumped into the bed, waiting for my little red riding hood.

"Send in Gisela. I'll summon you later."

"My lady?"

"Do as I order you!"

The door opened and shut with a click.

Gisela walked in with a pale face and bags underneath her eyes, showing how she had not recovered yet from her injury and infection. I wanted to pick her up and now properly nurse her back to health with rest and nutrition that she didn't receive on our journey back here.

I cared more for Gisela than I wanted to admit. Every time I saw her, I wanted to hug her. Just to show her that someone loved her. Yet another emotion played a vicious game of tug of war inside me. Doubt. Gisela had to compete with demons of my past and as unfair as that game was, it still was reality. I wanted to follow the Owl's advice, but blind trust wasn't in my nature as a warrior. Nor should it be with a prince and King.

Gisela's auburn hair lay about her shoulders and down her back slightly tangled. Her lack of height never made her diminutive in my eyes. Someone might mistake her for a little girl, especially in her red cloak. But I saw only the strength and fortitude she possessed in every fiber of her mind and body. All qualities that every princess and future queen required.

As she approached the bed and pulled back one side of the bed curtain she squinted at the darkness where I lay burrowed amongst the pillows. Of course, I was fooling Gisela again, but I had to one last time. I was going to be asking for a lot of forgiveness from her and God.

Her voice was thin and weak as she held the bedpost. "Are you alright Grandmama?

"Just a little under the weather."

"Your voice sounds different."

"It's just a little sore throat." I coughed trying to cover the deeper octave of my natural baritone.

"I've never seen you wear a shawl that way."

"I'm not well. I don't need your judgements."

She curled into herself like a turtle pulling its head into its' shell. I worried that I'd been too harsh but after a few moments she looked up again with a little more steel in her expression. "You wanted to see me Grandmama?"

"Sit down on the edge of the bed before you fall over."

She shivered and with each hand pulled the cloak ends around her and wrapped it tighter. She waited and sat there.

"Was your mission successful?"

She chewed her lower lip. "In a way."

"Explain yourself."

She cleared her throat. "We ... we did find the Owl in a manner of speaking."

"Either you did or did not." It was not easy to speak clipped sentences, but I had to make this act believable to Gisela. "What did he tell you?"

"That God had sent me a warrior. And that I must trust him."

"And do you?" My breath caught scared and eager to hear her answer.

#

Grandmama's question caught me completely off guard. Not only because her voice changed once again, but she never would have asked that question before. I peered harder at the figure shrouded in darkness, only a voice was decipherable. But the voice sounded so different from Grandmama's normal voice.

"I don't know who the warrior is."

"Maybe God wants you to trust the warrior as well as yourself."

I shake my head from the mental fog I struggled to escape. If it wasn't Grandmama, then who was it? The figure in the bed was bigger than her.

"What about the second task?"

I wanted to have this conversation when I was well, but if both of us were ill, then maybe Grandmama wouldn't react as poorly. With firm resolve I didn't want to lie outright. "I didn't find your red diamond."

"What do you mean, mine?"

"The red diamond is meant for the true ruler."

Her voice rose . "What do you mean true ruler?"

"Max is the true king. The red diamond is his alone."

"So, you *did* find it!" She harrumphed and I waited for an angry demand to hand it over. Instead, she sighed. "You sound confirmed in your answers. Didn't Max lie to us?"

"Yes, he did, but I forgive him."

"Shouldn't he be one to beg for forgiveness?"

"I hope he would apologize, but I still forgive him nonetheless, which is why I'll never be able to carry out your third request."

She doesn't respond right away. "My illness is making me a little forgetful what was my third request again."

No matter what illness she was fighting off, Grandmama would not have forgotten why she sent me out in the first place. I got off the bed, walked to the other end, and pulled back the bed curtain. The face framed by the shawl possessed different angles and the cheeks and chin sported whiskers. It was Max!

I folded my arms a little angry, but also fighting to not jump into his arms overjoyed that he was alive. "Why Grandmama how hairy you've gotten."

The guilt in his eyes transformed to amusement as he laughed, ripped off the shawl, and got up from the bed.

"How did you get here?"

"Marius, the wolves, Lena, and Selene released me and are taking over the castle."

"Where is Grandmama?"

"She's locked in a hope chest." He placed both hands on my shoulders and pulled me close. "Gisela, are you alright?"

Amidst thinking of all the other events occurring at this very moment I had forgotten about the last time we had seen each other and how I had narrowly cheated death. "I'll be alright..."

"But."

My mouth did not want to form the words. I didn't know how to explain the pain and doubt I experienced from his action. While also the love and fascination I also held for him. Including the prophecy from the Owl.

"I'd like to see Selene and Lena, before I'm put in the dungeon."

His eyebrows rose nearly to his hairline and questions filled his eyes. "What are you talking about?"

"I am Lady V's granddaughter."

He rolled his eyes. "Gisela, stop talking nonsense."

"Then what do you plan to do with me?"

He crossed his arms, and his brows furrowed. This was the Max I remembered, always fighting to control his annoyance with me. "I haven't decided yet. He paused and the sharp angles of his eyebrows softened. "I, first need to ask your forgiveness."

"Max, I already told you that I forgive you."

He took both my hands in his. Gently and sincerely. My fingers delicate in his. He stroked my fingers. My throat went dry, and my pulse zoomed like a hummingbird flitting around.

"I've been working to reclaim my kingdom from Lady V for most of my life. Marius and the wolves were my only family. We all wanted to avenge our families from her and the huntsmen. That never meant using you."

I tilted my head and raised my eyebrows.

"It's true. I did lie about my name but nothing else. Remember those pages you deciphered the day we left?"

I nodded.

"I tore those out of a book my grandfather left me."

"Wait! You tore pages out of a book?"

"That's not important right now. My point is that yes, I inadvertently gave you the pages to decipher, and then you found the red diamond." He reached into his pocket and pulled out the red diamond. "I found it while you were in the midst of your fever." He dropped it into my palm and folded my fingers over it. "I'm sorry that I took it from you." The pitch of voice softened.

I leaned closer to hear him.

"I worried that you were going to hide the diamond from me. Trust is not easy for me, but I realized that you were fighting a harder battle."

Our eyes locked. I bit my lip. I wanted him to know that I would listen with an open heart and mind.

"You always acted with integrity. The owl told me to trust you." He pulled my hand not holding the diamond to his lips. "And I do."

Hugo jumped from behind the doorway and grabbed me. He put a dagger to my neck. I hid my hands in my cloak and fumbled for a pocket to sequester the diamond.

Fury raged over Max's face, but his voice remained monotone. "Put down the dagger and I'll show you mercy."

"I've spent too long chasing you." He pressed the dagger deeper into my skin and I inhaled sharply. "Now where is the red diamond?"

Max folded his arms over his chest. "Aren't you worried about your patroness?"

"Don't play games with me. I'll slit her throat." He leaned closer. "Like I did her mother."

"What?" My heart broke knowing my mother perished in that gruesome manner.

"She arranged to meet with his father to share information to destroy Lady V's army. I arrived before them both." He pulled me back against him as Max took one step closer to us. "I wish I'd gotten to kill your father too, but his death from torture was well worth the wait later on."

"There's no where you can escape from this."

"True but I can take Gisela as collateral because you'll do anything for your little red won't you."

I peered at Max needing to know what he wanted me to. His attention was over Hugo's shoulder. His chin dipped and I heard a gong above me. Hugo crumbled with me to the floor.

Max pulled me out from underneath Hugo and wrapped me in his arms. His heartbeat raced next to my ear. In his arms was the warmest and most loving place I'd ever been.

Behind me someone sobbed, and I pulled out of Max's arms to see Selene holding both her hands up to her face as she wept. Down at her feet was a shovel. *Did she hit Hugo with that?*

I *walked over Hugo's comatose body to give comfort to my best friend, who had saved me.* But before I could Marius ran into the room and pulled Selene into his arms. I turned to look back at Max who shrugged with his hands up.

Across the room the hope chest thumped and moaned.

Max smiled at his men who had joined us. "Wolves, I think it's finally time to re-locate Lady V and the huntsmen temporarily to the dungeon."

"Then where will they go?" Grandmama deserved none of my concern, but I couldn't absolve all familial ties.

"Don't worry she'll love living in exile on an island with only a blind deaf mute to look after her."

\#

The ballroom glittered with freshly polished chandeliers, gleaming candlelight, and stirring music from the orchestra. Couples danced and courtiers chatted amongst the borders of the room. The night I had waited for. Coronation night.

The flurry of the last few days consuming every waking moment. Absolving the arcane laws. Dismissing bureaucrats who lined their pockets rather than serving the people. Clearing away all traces of the huntsmen and Lady V.

Finding no time to visit Gisela, I urged Lena and Selene to ensure that she finally rested and recovered from her fever. They sent daily written updates, but it paled in comparison to being in her presence.

It was my job to greet guests and appear composed. My mind and pulse were the opposite. If the court doctor knew my pulse kept time with the violinist, then he would have sent me to bed. *Where was Gisela?*

Lena and Selene came down the grand staircase where the wolves all greeted them and escorted them into the ballroom.

A hard slap on my back made me whirl around to see Marius there.

"You're going to scare the guests with that scowl."

"Then they can go home."

"You haven't been crowned king yet. Don't be surly."

"Don't you have someone else to bother?" I moved towards the stairs, when someone pulled back on my arm.

"Where do you think you're going?"

"I'm going up there to see what's taking her so long—"

Trumpets sounded and Gisela appeared at the top of the stairs in a gown of evergreen colored silk set off by her auburn hair falling in waves down her back. She'd always captivated my attention but the picture of her tonight I wanted—needed this image imprinted on my memory forever.

She bit her lip and looked down at the steps and back at me. *Was she nervous?* I leapt up the stairs, taking them two at a time to meet her. I bowed as she curtsied. I offered my arm to escort her down the rest of the way.

We got to the bottom of the stairs, and I signaled to the orchestra to resume playing.

"May I have this dance?" I held out my hand for her. She followed my lead around the dance floor and many watched our every movement. *Was it only weeks ago when I first held her in my arms for that dance?*

"You dance just like I remember." I whispered in her ear.

She peered up at me quizzically.

"I seem to recall you don't like flattery, but I've managed to gain your attention somehow."

She gasped. "That was you?"

"Guilty."

Her lips curl like she is begrudgingly amused. The musicians strum the last notes. We remain standing in same position as our arms slowly lower. "Am I forgiven?"

One corner of her mouth lifts. "Just as long as you remain Max."

I nodded and lead her outside away from the crowds. The cypress and olive groves should provide enough shelter from prying eyes.

Walking through the graveled pathways we reached a stone bench sandwiched between two cypress trees and sat down but I held on to one of her hands between my two. The speech I'd spent days practicing ready on lips only moments before, was now gone in the perfect setting under the stars and the moon. But I wouldn't miss this opportunity and spoke what had lived in my heart for days. "Those nights spent by the fire with you. I—. You—." I wanted to growl in frustration to not ruin this.

The sprightly music from the orchestra now replaced by the gentle tune of crickets singing to one another. I took a moment to regroup and gazed down at her hands inhaling the scent of jasmine and orange blossoms. I needed her to understand what she had done for me.

"That fire in you stoked my own for life. A life that I never considered. And now that flame, my red-headed beauty, burns only for you."

While still holding her hand, my other swept horizontally across the panorama. "This kingdom needs to be united and the only one I want by my side is you."

She shook her head, eyes downcast. "I don't think I'd be the right fit for you or to be the queen."

I knelt down on one knee as wanted her to know that even as King I will do whatever is in my power for her.

"I am, well, soon will be King, but also a man in love. When you told me what the Owl told you about God sending a warrior for you, I realized I wanted to be that warrior. And equally I hope you want to be that warrior for me."

A tear slid down her cheek. I brushed it away with my thumb.

"Will you have me as I am? Short tempered and grumpy."

She smiled with unshed tears in her eyes. "Only if you will have me as I am. Intelligent and impetuous."

My hands framed her face and I brought her close for a kiss. "My dear little red riding hood. This wolf wouldn't have it any other way."

The End

About the author

Kendall Hoxsey can be found amongst the vineyard rows in wine country dreaming up stories to hopefully find their way onto the page when she's not reading, cooking, or chasing after her two children and two French bulldogs. A lifelong lover of history, Kendall loves to weave her fascination with history into romantic historical tales. Luckily her own dashing hero husband provides plenty of inspiration.

Join her newsletter 'Tales from the Vine' to hear about upcoming projects.

Website: www.authorkendallhoxsey.com

Instagram: www.instagram.com/authorkendallhoxsey

Facebook: www.facebook.com/authorkendallhoxsey

Acknowledgements

Dear Reader,

    I hope you enjoyed reading A Noble Intent as much I enjoyed writing it! Coming out in February 2025, A Noble Collection, is an anthology of short stories by a few of the Cornerstone authors. Mine is about Marius and Selene's happily ever after using the fairytale of Snow White as inspiration. Also coming shortly will be a Special Edition of A Noble Intent! More time with Max and Gisela :-D As always thank you so much for taking the time to read something by an indie author. If you liked it please consider leaving a review.

    In January 2022 I took a writing class with MadLit Musings led by the 'sui generis' Jaime Jo Wright. Finally giving into the desire to write that I had kept stoking like an ember in my heart since I was twelve. From that point I've been on an incredible and blessed journey. In your hands/phone/e-reader is my third novella. With each experience I learn something about myself and the world around me.

    I've met so many incredible people along the way. They have welcomed me with open arms and for a budding writer that is invaluable.

To the Cornerstone Group- Thank you so much for the camaraderie. I've loved getting to read all the stories and thoroughly enjoyed this journey with you all!

To Eli- Oh dear Raven sis! Thank you. I hope you know how much I appreciate having you as my editor. You make each and every story so much better!

To Jaime-As always I'm so grateful to have you as a mentor and friend.

To my family thank you so much for your support. Especially to Jeff, Lizzie, and Jack. I love you three so much.

Also by Kendall Hoxsey

An Imminent Christmas Threat

Heart of Redemption

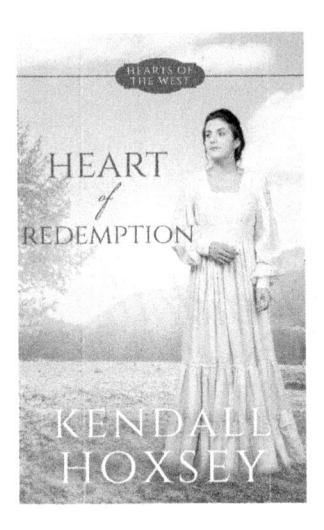

Made in the USA
Las Vegas, NV
12 February 2025